INTO THE EYE

To Barb

Best Wishes!

JOHN DOANE

Aventine Press

Published by Aventine Press
1023 4th Ave #204
San Diego CA, 92101
www.aventinepress.com

ISBN: 1-59330-446-3

Printed in the United States of America

To my friend, Barb,
who left us way too soon.

PROLOGUE

Darkness had settled over the Sunch'on valley and only a dusting of lights illuminated the missile launch complex that was about thirty-five miles north of Pyongyang. Deep below the ground's calm surface, however, banks of massive diesel generators powered a blinding array of halogen lamps that stood guard over skilled laborers working in nonstop shifts on the Taepodong-2X Intercontinental Ballistic Missile. The launch silo was over 160 feet deep, allowing the 105-foot long, three-stage missile enough room to have a protective blast door above it, and an exhaust collection and venting chamber below it. Technicians on a scaffolding near the topmost Third Stage finished the close-out checklist for the warhead compartment. Meanwhile, another group hastily worked out a low-pressure feed error with the fueling procedure of the First Stage. The diesel generators droned in a constant roar and filled the chamber with diesel fumes. This meant yelling was the only way to communicate, and coughing was as natural as the fatigue shared by the group.

In a soundproof booth above the sixth tier of the silo complex two men watched the work with complete focus. One wore a North Korean general's uniform and the other, taller by half a head, wore Aquascutum, and would not have looked out of place in Knightsbridge. They both appeared enthralled by the work on the highly secret missile.

Shooting his cuffs, the man said, "Will it be ready for launch on schedule?"

"Yes, Premier, we are almost done with the final checks. We will be ready," General Seong said, carefully keeping any tremor out of his voice. He was nervous about the highest ranking member of the Supreme People's Assembly visiting the launch complex but he had managed to push the staff at the launch complex hard enough to keep the missile's first test launch on schedule.

"It better be, General, for your sake," the Premier answered silkily. The people have worked very hard to bring us to this momentous occasion and I applaud the wise choice the Assembly made for the leader of this most important project," he said, his glance sliding over and fixing on Seong.

"Yes, Premier, of course! The launch will be on time and will be perfect," the general assured him. "Our ability to neutralize our enemies is almost at hand. The Taepodong-2X will have enough range to strike anywhere in the United States' mainland. They will see that we are not just another impotent, sandy oil tap. Then the Republic will take its rightful place as a true world power. I promise we will strike the Americans a deadly blow."

Premier Pak Pong Ju looked with casually concealed distaste at the sniveling flunky for a few painful seconds and then turned his gaze back to the missile. "Yes, we will."

CHAPTER 1

Lieutenant Commander AJ Connelly strained to see the whitecaps on the Sea of Japan through a small window in the Grumman turboprop. The midnight sea was choppy, giving the aircraft enough bounce that dozing was impossible.

After one particularly rough series of bumps, the copilot swiveled around and yelled back to Connelly over the din inside the cabin.

"Somebody needs to pave this damn road!" he shouted.

Connelly gave a distracted nod, his mind still on the gloom around them.

"I imagine you flew through some rough ones back on the *Ranger*, huh?" the lieutenant continued. Connelly smiled at the eagerness in the lieutenant's voice, which was not hidden by the drone of the engines.

"Yeah, we had our share of green water," Connelly replied.

"I know Jack Sanders," the lieutenant suddenly offered. The name of his old flying partner called up a flood of memories.

"He said you were one damn fine Tomcat pilot," the lieutenant continued.

"Good. The bribe is working," Connelly said lightly.

"What are you doing on the *Nimitz*? Rumor in the Ready Room is that you're carrier-qualifying a new ECM pod for the F-18. Is that right?"

Connelly paused for a moment since he had never heard that explanation for his trip to the aircraft carrier. For the last two years he had been sharing time between the Navy and the NSA. He usually flew 'unusual mission profiles' as they liked to call them, since 'get you killed missions' seemed to lower morale. Generally there was very little description of where he was going until he had flight clearance and this latest mission was no different. The cover story was, nevertheless, useful, whether it came from the NSA or the prolific rumor mill that exists onboard an aircraft carrier. At this point the lieutenant might be better informed than Connelly himself.

"Yeah, that's right. They want to see if the Hornet can still get off the deck with that banana slung under the fuselage. If it doesn't, maybe I can use it for something once I hit the water," he offered.

The lieutenant chuckled at Connelly's dry comments. Flying the Grumman E-2 on an "ass and trash run" was dull work and the lieutenant felt lucky to have some interesting conversation. It beat the senator's aide from last week who spent the whole trip on his blackberry.

An hour later, the pilot turned the E-2 sharply to the left across the bow of the *Nimitz,* which had suddenly appeared in the murky sea. Soon, they were on final approach, gaining on the carrier's fantail while sliding down an imaginary pipe that would deposit their aircraft on the steel deck. Even though Connelly had made hundreds of carrier landing as a pilot flying any one of seven different carrier-rated planes, each landing was thrilling, especially at night in poor weather. He looked out the window as the twin-engine plane rushed past the command 'island' and slammed onto the deck, signaling their arrival. The E-2 pilot had caught the third of the four arresting wires with the plane's tailhook which brought them to a sudden stop and threw everybody up against their harnesses. The violent screech marked it as a perfect carrier landing.

"Nice job," Connelly congratulated the pilot.

"Thank you, Sir," the lieutenant answered casually, hiding his rush of pride.

After taxiing to the assigned space, Connelly and the other passengers climbed out into the stormy night, ducking to avoid the wet slap of wind. Connelly jogged over to the island where the captain was waiting. Connelly threw up a swift salute which also shielded his eyes from the rain driving across the deck.

"Permission to come aboard?" Connelly shouted over the wind.

The captain answered him with a slap on the shoulder and ushered him inside. Once out of the storm, they brushed the water off of their sleeves and began walking down one of the familiar gray corridors.

"Welcome aboard, Commander," the Captain said.

"Thank you, Sir," Connelly said.

They continued silently through a series of corridors and down a couple of flights of stairs until they arrived at a closed door.

"Do you need a few minutes before the meeting?" the captain paused.

"No, I'm ready to go," Connelly replied mildly.

With a nod the captain punched the digits on the door's cipher lock and held the door as Connelly went inside.

It was one of the nicer briefing rooms on the carrier, with a wooden table in the middle and paneling to hide the steel bulkheads. In addition to the captain there were four other men in the room, one of them an Army general with three stars on his olive drabs and the other three notable for their civvies. The captain immediately began the introductions.

"Commander, this is Lieutenant General Marvin Arristol. He's from the Office of the Joint Chiefs of Staff and represents the President," he said, with no apparent deference. He pointed to the others as he introduced them.

"This is Mack Jurgensen from the NSA and these two gentlemen are Jim Barnes and Dave Straczynski from Palmdale."

Connelly had heard of Jurgensen since he was now working for the NSA but this was the first time he had met him. Jurgensen struck him as a typical manager, dressed in a Navy-blue pinstripe suit that obviously hadn't come off the rack. His blond hair showed no signs of thinning and his eyes no sign of warmth. What interested Connelly more was the presence of the two emissaries from Palmdale, the home of the Lockheed's famous 'Skunk Works' aircraft division. The Skunk Works had built the most advanced aircraft in the history of aviation, including the Mach 3+ SR-71, the F-117 Stealth Fighter, and since the 1950s had built a plane which Connelly had been flying quite a bit lately- the high-altitude U-2 reconnaissance jet. Connelly prided himself on his ability to remain unimpressed, but he felt something like intrigue stir at the back of his mind.

After pausing to allow Connelly a chance to shake hands, the captain then gestured for everyone to sit around the table. An aide took out a stack of black folders, passed one to each man at the table, and then silently left the room.

"Gentlemen, this is now a classified briefing. The contents of this folder and the discussion about to take place are top secret and the usual nondisclosure rules apply."

Given the guest list, Connelly was not surprised at all that this operation was not for public consumption. Everyone pulled the briefing papers out of their folders and opened them.

"You now hold the details of *Operation Blacklight.* Its purpose is to ascertain the development level and numerical presence of intercontinental ballistic missiles in North Korea," the captain began. He then gestured to Jurgensen to continue the discussion.

"The NSA has been quietly gathering information for over a year, of course, the closed nature of North Korea makes this very difficult. Approximately two months ago an attempt was made to conduct a fly-over of the suspected sights but it failed."

General Arristol jumped in at this point.

"We launched a U-2 out of Osan and it got nailed the second it crossed the border. There are SA-6 sites all over the border and they launched at least seven missiles at the recon plane. The first four were defeated but the plane got nailed by the fifth. The pilot was killed and the plane destroyed."

Connelly had heard that a US aircraft had been lost in South Korea but the published reports said it was a P-3 Orion on a weather flight and that it had crashed because of mechanical difficulties. It made more sense now that he knew the truth. Arristol continued.

"It is of grave importance to the President that this mission be completed. Our efforts on the ground and otherwise have been very slow and unproductive. The North Koreans have the satellite tracks practically memorized and they are very good at hiding things when the satellites pass overhead. It will take too long to change their orbits sufficiently to surprise the North Koreans and the information is needed now."

Jurgensen then took over again.

"Obviously, the North Koreans are watching flights coming out of the South with sharp eyes and they don't give a damn about diplomatic consequences of shooting down aircraft. Most of their surveillance radars are positioned on the border and around the western perimeter of the country. They track anything that's approaching and move their mobile SAM launchers as necessary," he explained very seriously.

Connelly began to wonder how they were going to get a successful overflight given the well-supplied and hostile stature across the border. Jurgensen then proceeded to explain the concept behind *Blacklight*.

"The only weakness we have found in their defenses is that due to a terrible infrastructure their power grid is very limited. They also have a top-heavy bureaucracy that is slow to respond. Our previous intelligence suggests that if an aircraft *suddenly* appeared from the northeast they would have trouble responding to it. Apparently a number of phone calls have to be made and some signed documents delivered by horseback. I'm not kidding. Then they have to hook up their mobile fire control radars and move them behind a truck. The mobile SAMs soon follow behind."

Connelly nodded a little bit as he started to put together the plan in his head. He understood where he was going to fit into the picture but the two men from the Skunk Works and their meeting on an aircraft carrier still didn't click. Jurgensen then laid it out for him.

"Any flights coming from Alaska or other bases far away allow them enough time to cover up their facilities. However, our estimates predict that it would take them two hours and five minutes to respond in a hostile fashion to a sudden, northeasterly penetration of their airspace. This gives us the opportunity to get a U-2 over the suspected missile site before they can cover it up, and back out again before they start firing," he stated dramatically.

Connelly began to realize what they had in mind and thought to himself that it didn't sound like such a great idea...

Captain Gainesville then interjected,"So, that's what the boys from Lockheed are doing here and why their crates are taking up half of my hangar deck!"

Jurgensen nodded and continued, "Yes, the team from the Skunk Works is going to assemble the U-2 that's been delivered to this carrier. Then—"

Jurgensen was interrupted by Connelly who, at this point, had a broad smile on his face, the kind a boy puts on when he realizes his leg is being pulled.

"You're telling me that they're going to try to assemble a U-2 on board this ship? It's here in pieces, in many crates? Is that right?" he asked with considerable skepticism.

Jay Barnes, the lead engineer from the Skunk Works team, shifted uneasily in his seat and then spoke up.

"Yes, Sir. Tom and I have trained with a team we brought from Palmdale to be able to assemble the ship in the field, or on the sea in this case. We've brought all of the assembly and alignment jigs that we'll need."

Connelly was intimately familiar with the design and construction of the U-2 and knew how difficult and demanding the assembly process was. His visits to Plant 42 impressed on him the level of precision and craftsmanship required to build this extraordinary airship. The thought of putting one together anywhere besides the plant was hard to swallow. Yet, that's what they were proposing.

"OK, so it's May sixteenth today; when do we fly? November?" he asked sarcastically.

Jurgensen was not taking Connelly's irreverent attitude very well and cast a sideways look at him.

"Are you up for this, Commander?" Jurgensen asked with his eyes locked on Connelly.

Connelly took a long drink from a glass of water and stared back at Jurgensen. After a few seconds of tense silence, Connelly looked down at the table and drummed his fingers on it. He then looked over at Barnes and addressed them, purposefully ignoring Jurgensen.

"Can you and your boys put this thing together?" he asked earnestly.

Barnes, who admired all pilots who flew Lockheed products, swallowed a bit roughly. He cleared his throat and replied.

"Yes, Sir, Commander Connelly. We can do it."

Connelly nodded several times, folded his arms across his chest, and glared back at Jurgensen.

"Yeah, I'm up for it. My buddy here says he can put my plane together right and that's all I need to know. When do we light the fire?"

Captain Gainesville was acutely aware of the tension in the room and decided to pour a little cold water on it. He cleared his throat loudly.

"Here's the order: tomorrow, at dusk, I'll launch two fighter patrols and a refueler. Then we'll begin moving the jigs onto the flight deck. I don't like fouling my deck but I realize how important this is. You can set up just forward of the island on the starboard side. The starboard elevator is at your disposal. While you're doing this I can't launch anything from the bow catapults but, at some point, I'll need to recover the fighter patrols so you can't use the waist area."

General Arristol took over at this point.

"It's important to do all of this under the cover of darkness. The Korean reconnaissance patrols, thinly disguised as fishing vessels, keep a pretty tight watch on the carrier battle group. They would get suspicious if they saw us setting this stuff up and they'd call central command the second they recognized the Dragon Lady," he said, using the affectionate term given to the U-2. He continued, "It's imperative that we launch before daylight."

Connelly struck a wide smile and pursed his lips tightly. If it took months in Palmdale to assemble a plane, how were they going to do it in one night? It seemed impossible but, then again, most of what the Skunk Works accomplished seemed impossible.

"The sun sets about seven p.m.," Captain Gainesville added. "Your flight needs to be feet-wet by sunrise at five-o-nine a.m. That's a ten hour window which means that, allowing an hour for launch, you've got seven hours to assemble the aircraft. In the dark."

The Captain leaned back in his chair, obviously beginning to share Connelly's skepticism about the time table. Barnes straightened up in his chair.

"Yes Sir. It's tight, but we've rehearsed this scenario a dozen times. At Palmdale we simulated the conditions by turning off the lights in the main assembly bay, piping in simulated ocean sound and vapor spray, and using nothing that wasn't in the tool lockers we've brought on board this week. On our last practice run we completed the assembly in six hours and forty minutes."

"Well, that leaves enough time for a quick wash and wax!" Connelly added to the amusement of no one but himself.

"Commander, you'll be briefed on the details of the mission tomorrow. We'll wake you for flight prep and have you ready to go in time. The rest is up to you, Barnes," the captain stated.

The meeting was dismissed and everyone left the room in silence. Connelly figured that this mission was unlikely to succeed but had never stopped him before, especially when it seemed that the benefits were worth it. He took a stroll around the carrier and talked to a few officers with whom he was acquainted. It had been a long day so he retired shortly thereafter.

The next morning he had breakfast in the main galley and spent the morning leisurely contemplating the mission ahead. After lunch he went to the special briefing room and sat down with two officers from the ship's highly classified mission planning division. Over the course of several hours he absorbed the mountains of information being presented to him. There were flight routes, terrain identifiers, weather information, and fuel burn rates, not to mention the short-course in North Korean military status. It was a lot of information but he was gifted at compiling tremendous amounts of data for recall later. He asked a few questions about operational details and then headed back to his cabin for some sleep. He would be awoken in the middle of the night and wanted to get a decent amount of rest.

The minute the sun set behind the fantail of the supercarrier, Barnes and his crew rushed to get the aircraft parts and all their tools onto the main deck. Even though launch was eight hours away Barnes felt the value of each minute and knew he couldn't spare even one. The nine technicians he had brought with him from the Lockheed plant were the best and they all carried out their duties with lightning speed and brain-surgeon-like precision. The bunks for holding the fuselage were locked down to the steel deck of the carrier and the the wings positioned on pylons. There was a footlocker full of cables and hoses that had to be connected to various parts inside the wing running through to the fuselage. Each connector had to be properly assembled and each hose fitted tightly. The darkness and the occasional sea spray slowed things down since they couldn't see everything but knew that the saltwater had to be wiped off before it caused problems. Barnes ran the operation with the deft hand of an orchestra conductor and was spared no dirt on his clothes. The sound of ratchets and air hoses flowed across the deck as the team worked their magic in the night.

At midnight a rap on the cabin door woke Connelly. A seaman opened the door slightly and stuck his head in.

"Excuse me, Commander. I was told to wake you at twenty-four hundred hours," he explained politely.

Connelly quickly put his feet on the floor and wiped his eyes.

"Thanks, Chief," he answered.

After a quick shower he put on a pair of dark blue trousers and a gray t-shirt. For this mission there would be no uniform, no cap or hat, no identification of any kind. It was that kind of a mission. He made his way to the temporary physiological support area set up for him. He ate the standard high-protein meal of eggs and steak and then sat down while the flight surgeon looked him over. Once he was authorized for the flight he began the laborious process of putting on the space suit required for flying the U-2. Since the Dragon Lady flew so high it was necessary to wear a suit that would protect him in the event he had to leave the aircraft at a high altitude where the air was very thin and very cold.

It took twenty minutes to get his legs into the lower portion of the suit and into his special boots. The technicians helped him into the upper part of the suit and they made sure it was sealed properly. Once the suit was checked out he laid down on a reclining bench and stuck the oxygen supply mouthpiece between his lips. For the next two hours he would breathe pure oxygen to filter the nitrogen out of his bloodstream. Just like diving, a pilot ejecting at high altitude could suffer the potentially fatal effects of 'the bends' if there was nitrogen in his blood.

Two hours later, Connelly got up with the help from the technicians and fitted his space helmet on. Once sealed, a flow of pure oxygen was delivered into the helmet from a portable tank that he was now carrying. It was awkward getting from the physiological support area to the flight deck since it involved climbing two flights of stairs and turning a number of very tight turns which was quite a challenge in the space suit. Nevertheless he made it and he glanced at his watch before looking out onto onto the flight deck. Gainesville had set a deadline of three a.m. for Barnes to be finished. It was two fifty-eight a.m. and Connelly could see through the dim light on the flight deck that Barnes was smiling as he rubbed the U-2's cockpit windscreen with a cloth.

"Two coats of wax- she's ready to go!" he shouted across the deck.

Connelly couldn't help but chuckle at Barnes. He strode over to the airship and made a slow walk-around in astonishment at what they had accomplished. It was difficult to talk through the visor on the helmet so Connelly simply put his hand on Barnes' shoulder and patted it a couple of times. The Lockheed engineer knew exactly what the Navy officer was trying to convey and smiled with a deep sigh of relief.

"Well, let's help you get in," Barnes offered and he, along with two technicians, helped Connelly get into the cockpit. It took quite a while to get him strapped in and make all the adjustments necessary for flight. Barnes went over some of the peculiarities of this 'article', as they called an individual U-2, and showed him some limitations of the assembly. The reconnaissance suite was designed largely for this mission and Barnes spent some time explaining the interface to Connelly.

Eventually they were ready and a technician started the Pratt and Whitney J75 engine. Once it stabilized at idle speed, they transferred all of Connelly's physiological support to the onboard systems and took the portable gear with them. Connelly checked the clock on the instrument panel: four forty eight a.m. Twenty-one minutes left. "Truly amazing," he muttered to himself. Barnes closed the canopy over him and checked to make sure it sealed properly. Once everything looked right, he gently slapped his hand a couple of times on the Plexiglas canopy and gave Connelly the thumbs-up signal. Connelly gave him a salute which, since Barnes was a civilian, was inappropriate, but it filled the Lockheed engineer with a deep sense of pride. He was proud to be part of the mission.

He left the flight deck and headed into the island with the rest of his crew. They went up a deck and watched the beautiful Dragon Lady from the first-floor balcony. Even though the Nimitz was some 250 feet across at her widest, the 100 foot wingspan of the U-2 made the ship seem thin. Connelly pushed the throttle ahead just slightly and the U-2 gracefully rolled away from her parking spot. The 'pogos', a pair of spring-loaded supports underneath each wing, flexed and recovered as the U-2 moved forward on her tandem pair of wheels. The pitching and rolling of the carrier deck made the plane's taxi look odd, since it was never intended to operate this way.

By the time Connelly had squared up the plane, the bulk of the Nimitz's air wing pilots were gathered on several of the island's balconies. This was quite a spectacle and one not to be missed. The takeoff alone would be 'worth the price of admission' since the U-2 was not designed to take advantage of the steam-powered catapult used to accelerate other aircraft to flying speed before they slipped over the bow of the mighty ship. Connelly was going to have to get the aircraft airborne in approximately 1,000 feet! He got some help when Captain Gainesville turned the *Nimitz* into the wind and ordered flank speed. With the eleven knots of sea breeze added to the ship's thirty-three knot speed, Connelly was spotted a forty-four knot head start. The U-2 could fly at seventy-eight knots so he thought he could get airborne before the short steel deck disappeared behind him.

"Dragon Five, this is Home Plate," came the voice of Captain Gainesville over the radio.

"Dragon Five here," replied Connelly using the code name given to him for this flight.

"The flight deck is all yours- you are clear for takeoff at your discretion," he informed Connelly.

"Roger that," was the reply.

Even though he had the whole 1,030-foot length of the *Nimitz's* deck to work with he planned for a maximum-performance takeoff. During preflight planning he had calculated how long the takeoff run would take and made some rough measurements of how much time elapsed between up-swings and down-swings of the ship's bow. He wanted to time his takeoff so that he would pass over the bow at its peak, getting a little boost upward and having a few extra feet between him and the cold, black sea water.

He double-checked the dials and indicators showing that the U-2 was ready for launch. He pushed down on the foot pedals to engage the wheel brakes as he gripped the throttle and edged it forward until it was set at full power. The J75 whistled and whined at 12,000 RPM, the brakes straining to hold back the Dragon Lady. Connelly watched the artificial horizon on his instrument panel to gauge the up and down pitching of the carrier deck and, when it was at the precise point he had calculated, he let go of the brakes.

The lightweight reconnaissance plane pushed Connelly back into his seat as it picked up speed racing down the deck. He concentrated on the exact line he needed to follow in order to safely pass the island. The small tires bumped as he crossed over the various catapult grooves and access panels in the deck. Halfway down the deck the bow was pointed down into the water and Connelly hoped his calculations were right. As he sped towards the bow he kept his eyes on the instrument panel watching the pitch angle of the aircraft and the climbing airspeed.

The bow of the mighty carrier pushed upwards and, a mere ten feet from the front edge of the ship, the U-2 broke contact with the deck and launched into the dark night. He couldn't see the surface of the water for lack of moonlight, so he used his instruments to put the aircraft into a slight climb. Once the airspeed increased he pulled back on the control yolk and the nimble jet began pitching upward, now gaining altitude rapidly.

It only took a few minutes to attain the designated altitude of 10,000 feet. He leveled off and pulled the throttle back considerably to arrest the jet's vertical speed.

"Dragon Five, this is Starlight Lead. Are you up here?" came a voice over the radio.

"Yeah, I'm here. The boys back in Palmdale might find some sushi in the wheel wells later, but I made it," he replied.

"Roger on the sushi," came the reply from the pilot of the three-plane group of reconnaissance turboprops forming up on him.

The U-2 was trying to slip into their formation to look like a part of the normal four-ship flight that had been ferreting the North Korean border for the past couple of weeks. The U-2 was never intended to fly in formation and their pilots never practiced it. Despite thousands of hours of formation flying in other aircraft it was a challenge to keep the jet tucked in with the turboprops. Connelly needed a few minutes to get the feel of keeping this jet positioned correctly, especially since a pair of red and white navigation lights were all he could use.

It took about thirty minutes to reach the turn where Connelly would separate from the formation and head off on his solo mission.

"All right, Dragon Five, this is the bus stop. We're heading back to the castle. Have a good flight," came the call from the turboprop.

"Thanks for the dance, guys. See you later," Connelly replied.

The P-3 turboprops banked left into a sharp turn and Connelly turned ten degrees to the right and pushed the throttle forward to its maximum setting. As the P-3s lumbered back towards the safety of South Korean airspace, Connelly's U-2 rocketed up through the atmosphere. 20,000 feet came and went in a matter of minutes as did 30,000 feet and 40,000 feet. He monitored the altimeter closely and cross-checked the engine's turbine inlet and outlet temperatures to make sure he wasn't climbing too slowly or too quickly. Everything looked good as he passed through 50,000 feet.

As he continued to climb, the air outside the sleek black jet got thinner and thinner. With less air to create lift, the long, slender wings on the U-2 had to work harder to keep the aircraft climbing. The extreme aerodynamic conditions placed the U-2 in a precarious position: either a stall or a 'mach buffet' would cause the jet to flip out of control and pinwheel towards the ground. In most cases the only thing capable of arresting this descent was the ground. At Connelly's final cruising altitude, 76,000 feet, this 'coffin corner' of the flight envelope was only four knots wide. He carefully adjusted the throttle as he made the first turn, now over North Korean soil.

In a small radar shack on the Pukch'ong peninsula, two North Korean soldiers sat with their feet up on a table. One of them, an avid ping pong player, was bouncing a dirty white ping pong ball off of the olive green colored cabinet housing their Dnestr-M radar display.

"So, you think you can beat Tong?" Yongjik asked the ping pong player.

"Of course! He is not that good. I beat him two years ago at the Haiphong tournament. I can beat him again!" Sungmun said confidently.

"Yes, you did beat him then, but he was only eight years old. He is ten now!" howled Yongjik.

Just as Sungmun threw the ball at his taunting friend, a warning buzzer erupted in the shack as a red light also started blinking, indicating a sudden target on the radar.

"What the hell? Where did that come from?" Yongjik shouted rhetorically.

"I don't know! The radar must have malfunctioned. There's no way we could not have seen this target for the last hundred miles! It's somewhere above 50,000 feet..." Sungmun began muttering as he turned dials and punched buttons on the console, trying to tune the radar system to get more accurate readings of the jet's position.

"I will notify command," Yongjik said as he grabbed the handset from the telephone. After a few minutes he was connected to the regional commander, Major Yun, to whom he explained the sudden appearance of the radar contact.

"What do you mean it just appeared?!" the major shouted in exasperation. "We are in the middle of conducting our missile test! This is unacceptable!" the commander shouted at the lowly soldier. "You will be executed for your incompetence! Why didn't you see it earlier? Were you asleep?!" he continued and then suddenly hung up.

In the missile command center, the major scurried across the control center and quickly saluted a general.

"General Seong, I have terrible news! An incompetent radar surveillance crew in the Hungnam sector just reported a radar target! I will have them executed immediately!" he said.

The general's face grew dark as he absorbed the implications of an aircraft, most likely a surveillance jet, violating their airspace at this most critical juncture of their test. They were in the process of preparing their first Taepodong-2X for launch testing. It was a most critical moment for the advancement of their offensive military capability and all eyes in P'yongyang were watching.

"We must destroy the aircraft immediately," General Seong ordered with a tone of voice incongruent with his anxiety level.

"Yes Sir!" Major Yun blurted out. He continued, "We will scramble an SA-6 unit immediately!"

Yun then ran across the room again and started barking orders at a lieutenant who was shocked by the news and the major's threats if he failed. A quick analysis of the intruder's flight path pointed to a location where the SA-6 unit could set up to intercept the jet. An order was quickly issued to the SAM depot in Hungnam where a lieutenant and an enlisted solider ran out to their storage warehouse and turned the crank on a fifty-year-old truck with a thirty-year old missile unit hitched to it. After a minute of grinding and coughing, the Soviet-built truck blasted to life with a large, thick black cloud of smoke and the piercing sound of shearing metal. Despite being run once a month, the condition of the truck was terrible, reflecting the poor state of maintenance in the North Korean military. The enlisted man, Corporal Kim, needed all his strength to push the clutch pedal in and then all his abdominal strength to force the gear shift lever into first gear. With a guttural grinding and ear-piercing shriek, the old truck lurched forward, yanking the missile launcher with it.

They headed down a pothole-ridden dirt road with Lieutenant Park constantly looking behind him to make sure the SAM unit hadn't disconnected from the truck. So far, so good.

"Sir, where are we going?" Corporal Kim asked.

"You don't need to know!" shouted Lieutenant Park, annoyed at his subordinate for asking about classified information.

"Yes Sir, I understand, but I need to know if we are to go right or left at this intersection," he explained.

Lieutenant Park, wanting to slap the enlisted man for no other reason than pointing out that he himself was an idiot, chose to suppress his embarrassment and told the driver to turn left to get to the intercept point.

Shortly after crossing over the beach, Connelly engaged the cameras and began recording visual images of military points of interest below. The port of Hungnam had several ships in it that were clearly used for military purposes and the railroad tracks leading in and out had some cars on them. The intelligence guys back in Washington could gain some valuable information from the status of rail traffic taken during a time in which the North Koreans knew that no satellite was watching them.

Cellulose and electronic images were being captured every few seconds as Connelly made his way towards the major target- the suspected secret ICBM site at Yangdok. A GPS fix and a star check confirmed his navigation and showed that he was now only thirty-eight minutes away. He felt a slight tingle in his toes.

"Here! Here! Stop!" shouted Lieutenant Park.

Corporal Kim mashed his foot on the truck's brake pedal which caused the rusty brake shoe to rub against the corroded drum causing little more effect than to produce a shrill sound. The truck stopped basically because Kim steered it into a ditch.

Park jumped out of the truck and began yelling at Kim to deploy the SA-6. The corporal leapt out of the truck and ran to the hitch, where he began lowering the foot by turning a crank.

"What are you doing?" yelled Park.

"I must disconnect the launcher from the truck so that the exhaust won't destroy the truck!" he replied in an exasperated tone.

"Forget the truck- we only have a few minutes. Get the system working!"

Kim exhaled quickly, saluted the lieutenant, and turned the key to start the generator on the SA-6. The portable diesel generator for the radar was in much better condition than the truck and had no trouble starting up. Kim expertly ducked into the tiny cubicle where the fire-control radar screen was located. He pushed a number of buttons that activated the various servos and hydraulic pumps used to run the mobile SAM. It took a couple of minutes for the radar to warm up and begin its sky search. As he was scanning for the intruder, he proceeded with the pre-launch sequence knowing that, one way or the other, Lieutenant Park was going to fire this missile.

A red light illuminated on Connelly's threat board, indicating that a mobile SAM fire control radar had activated. He kept an eye on it as he proceeded towards Yangdok.

Six minutes later, Kim had located the high-flying jet on the search radar.

"Where is it?" Park asked anxiously.

"It is directly overhead right now!" Kim replied.

"Fire the missile! Shoot it down!" Park barked like a child.

Although Kim had not had time to obtain a solid radar-lock on the target, he knew that Park was at his limit and he had to do something. Kim flipped a switch that overrode the fire control radar's lock-on requirement which allowed him to fire the missile without having a solid signal. The SA-6 normally took one point five seconds to leave the launcher after the main motor ignited. Kim was worried as it stretched past three seconds since he had pressed the manual launch button. He heard some hissing and low rumbling and, much to his relief, the main motor finally igniting. The partially corroded wiring in the SAM launcher was barely able to ignite the old propellent in the motor and barely did. The 1,400 pound missile roared off the launch rail and, as he predicted, smothered the old truck in rocket exhaust, tearing the doors off and setting it on fire. Kim hoped that their radio was still working so that they would not have to walk back to their base.

A second red light flashed on Connelly's control panel and a buzz sounded in his helmet, alerting him to the SAM launch. He located it on the sensing board and then visually spotted it in his downward-pointing periscope. The telltale white dot began a spiraling path that indicated a SAM in flight. The fact that it did not change location in his viewer meant that it was tracking him perfectly.

Ten seconds into its flight, the first stage motor was almost exhausted. A switch in the motor was supposed to ignite the second stage and carry the explosive payload to its target. This SA-6 was old and the switch had corroded to the point where it did not function at all. When the first stage burnt out, the SAM's mighty roar quickly faded and the only sound it was producing came from the air whooshing past the control fins. The battery in the SAM's guidance unit, remarkably, still worked. However, steering the control fins was pointless as the missile's speed fell to zero and it began to nose over back towards the ground.

Lieutenant Park had sat down on the ground and lit a cigarette, relieved to know that he had done his part as the major had ordered. Corporal Kim, on the other hand, had stayed at the control screen and became alarmed when he saw the error light indicating the missile's motor failure. He jumped out of the control booth and looked up into the sky. He saw the last flickers of the first stage motor as it burned out directly overhead and he could see that the missile was returning from its shortened journey. He felt no compunction to warn the lieutenant as he took off running down the road. He estimated twelve seconds for the missile to return to terra firma and, when he counted to eight in his head, leapt into the drainage ditch and wrapped his arms around his head.

The SA-6 impacted the ground about five meters from the launcher. Lieutenant Park only heard the whoosh a few seconds before the impact and had no time to react. Although the warhead did not detonate, the motor fuel and shrapnel created an impressive explosion that destroyed the mobile launcher and burned for almost an hour. Kim had to walk home.

The second the SAM warning light went out on his panel, Connelly returned his full attention to the flight path and made sure the cameras were running. He was only eight minutes from Yangdok.

In the ICBM command center, General Seong asked for the status of the intruder.

"The mobile SAM failed. The jet is six minutes away," Major Yun replied.

The general slowly but deliberately walked towards the major.

"Major Yun, if that jet flies over this facility, I will have you shot at sunrise. Is that clear?"

The major's face turned white since he knew that General Seong never made idle threats. Yun tried desperately to think of a way to intercept the aircraft and save his own life. The only fighter aircraft available were a pair of Mig-25s that were too far away to be of help. He put his hands on the desk to steady himself as he racked his brain for ideas. Then he had it.

Connelly's cameras were now recording images of the Yangdok missile complex. He could see the infrared camera's display in real time and saw that there was a tremendous amount of activity at the missile complex. Clearly, the ICBM development was the focus of the North Korean war machine's efforts. There were trucks and trains all over the place and, from the infrared signature, had been running very recently. The power grid showed up easily and indicated electrical service unseen anywhere else in the country's power grid. Not only was this place active, it was *very* active. Connelly knew that the intelligence he was gathering would startle everyone in Washington, all the way up to the president's office. He made sure the cameras and recorders were operating properly and, assured they were, he checked his navigation and continued to view the startling scene in his periscope.

Major Yun, his eyes wide open, walked solemnly to a man who was seated at the main control panel for the ICBM.

"Captain Namgung, shoot down that jet," he said with no emotion in his voice.

The captain turned his head and looked at the major.

"Sir?" he inquired.

"You heard me- shoot down that jet," Yun said with a rising voice.

"With what?" came the question form the perplexed launch officer.

The major didn't speak- he simply pointed to the ICBM control panel. The captain didn't understand at first. His face contorted as he tried to discern what the major was suggesting.

"This is the control panel for the ballistic missile," he explained, hoping that Yun had become confused in the excitement.

Yun simply stared at him, square in the face and said nothing.

"You're not suggesting I fire the ICBM at it, are you?" he asked incredulously.

"Captain, hit that jet. That is an order," Yun said.

The captain shrugged his shoulders and turned his hands palm-up.

"This isn't a SAM! I can't hit a jet with it!" he said in an exasperated tone.

"We can eventually build another missile but we could never rebuild the secrecy we presently have regarding this missile," the major explained.

He then glanced at General Seong whose glare was almost lethal.

The major then pulled his 9mm pistol from its holster and pointed it at the captain's head. The captain's pulse immediately doubled and his fingers trembled as he put them randomly on the control panel.

"But Sir, I have no tracking radar slaved to this missile!" he cried out.

The only response he got was the cocking of the hammer on the pistol.

The captain started to cry as he frantically started pressing buttons, at first in blind, random order, simply trying to look like he was doing something in order to keep the major from killing him. After a few seconds he was able to collect his senses and begin thinking. The major was serious and no one was going to stop him, so the captain tried to think of a way to hit the tiny jet with this huge missile that was designed to fly thousands of miles and hit a city. He was able to tie in one of the facility's search radars and he located the intruder. He projected the ICBM's flight path over the display and saw that the planned path to Washington, D.C., would take the missile away from the jet's location. He knew that, fortunately, the missile was fueled and its pre-launch procedure completed, so the missile would leave the silo about fifteen seconds after he pressed the big red button on his console. Considering that delay, he searched the list of preprogrammed targets and found one in India whose trajectory would intersect the jet's flight path. He pulled a roll of charts out from under his desk and quickly flipped through them, pulling out the right one. It showed the vertical trajectory of the missile on a flight of the right distance. He made some very quick calculations in his head to determine what altitude the missile would have when it crossed paths with the blip on the search radar. It would be close. He hated the idea of launching such a valuable missile with so little preparation but he, like Corporal Kim a few minutes ago, knew that his survival and not firing the missile were mutually exclusive conditions. He hurriedly scribbled calculations on the desk trying to figure out when to launch the missile. He knew that his window of opportunity was shrinking but he could sense the muzzle of the pistol only a few inches from the back of his head and it motivated him to perform calculations as fast as a supercomputer. He laid the track onto the screen and made marks on the radar display with his grease pencil and adjusted it twice. He smeared a mark onto the glass screen, indicating the point in the jet's progress at which he would initiate the launch.

Connelly had passed over Yangdok and was happy with the seemingly flawless collection of 'intel'. The cameras kept running even though the prime target had been surveyed. His flight plan called for a thirty degree left turn in twenty-five seconds. Suddenly the missile launch indicator illuminated on his panel, accompanied by the buzzing in his helmet. Oddly, there had been no fire-control radar lock buzzer. He looked down into the periscope again and steered it around looking for the SAM and quickly located it.

"OK, there it is," he murmured to himself in his helmet. He had visually acquired the SAM which normally made him feel a little better but, for some reason, it made his stomach tighten this time.

"Man, that's a serious first stage on that baby," he again said into his helmet.

"Christ, that thing's a big mother. It's bigger than any damn SAM I've ever seen... It's as big as a—" he didn't finish his sentence as his mouth went dry. Realizing that the ICBM had been fired at *him*, he scoured his imagination for a course of action. His first thought was that the ballistic missile couldn't possibly hit him since it was not designed to intercept *aircraft*- it was designed to obliterate cities. Nevertheless, the unwavering white spot grew larger in his periscope as the gargantuan missile roared higher into the atmosphere. Connelly considered evasive maneuvers to evade the missile but he was pinned into the U-2 flight envelope's 'coffin corner' which allowed him very little room to do anything. He did what he could, which was to initiate a shallow turn to the left and reduce power as he started the most rapid descent he could under the conditions. The U-2 nosed over slightly and began to descend.

Concentrating with brain-surgeon like intensity, the Korean captain watched the seconds tick off on the launch clock, indicating the elapsed time since the missile had left the silo. At precisely sixteen point three seconds he would activate the auto-destruct mechanism, detonating the missile. He hoped it would be at the right altitude.

Connelly could now see the blowtorch-like plume propelling the ICBM upwards. As it closed on him with ever increasing speed he thought it might just miss him. As it got closer it was harder to follow since its speed was quite high. He saw it flash in front of him, maybe a hundred yards away. In the millisecond he had to think, he worried that the turbulence from the rocket exhaust might be enough to upset the fragile stability of his jet. His concern for the exhaust turbulence evaporated as the missile detonated in a blinding flash of light. Even though his space helmet's visor protected his vision some, the exploding missile lit up the sky so brilliantly that he had to close his eyes. A few seconds later, the shock wave generated by the tremendous explosion reached his aircraft. The starboard wing flipped up immediately and the craft was thrown into an inverted spin. The rush of air backwards across the engine inlet disrupted the flow enough to stall the engine- a loud bang made its way into Connelly's ears as the compressor vomited its high-pressure air back out the inlet.

Inside the cockpit, no less than five warning lights were flashing and a cacophony of buzzers were going off. As the jet began falling through the atmosphere Connelly knew he was in trouble. The U-2 was notorious for trapping any pilot who got it into a spin, and no one had ever recovered one from an *inverted* spin. His body was now suspended by the harness on his seat and the lights on the ground spun lazily 'above' him. He knew that the U-2 was not structurally built for aerobatics and the stresses on the airframe were probably above their design tolerances already. He figured that even if the wings stayed on, he was in deep shit since the engine couldn't be restarted until he descended to about 30,000 feet where the air density was high enough to initiate a restart. At that point he would no doubt be in the sights of a dozen SAM launchers and every Mig the North Koreans could get airborne. He had to make a decision and the least evil of all the choices still made his stomach turn.

Even though he knew that the photographic reconnaissance he had accumulated that night was of inestimable value, it would be worse for the enemy to get their hands on it and reveal the state of the art in reconnaissance. Connelly reached under the instrument panel and released a protective cover that exposed a red handle. He grasped the handle, pulled it out, twisted it, and pushed it back in. A new light illuminated on the instrument panel, one confirming that the self-destruct charge had been activated which, after a ten minute fuse expired, would result in an explosive detonation that would destroy all of the U-2's vital parts. With that taken care of, he secured the wires, cables, and other umbilicals connecting him to the aircraft. He then grasped the ejection handles between his feet and yanked the black and yellow cords towards his chest. He heard the click and momentary hiss before the canopy exploded away from him, propelled by small charges. Then the Martin-Baker ejection seat's rocket motor blasted into action, firing Connelly out of the cockpit with a sledgehammer-like force.

The initial downward trajectory took Connelly away from the jet for a few seconds and then the seat's automatic guidance system began to steer the seat upward so that it was gaining altitude. Connelly grunted under the strain of a dozen g's and he began to black out as the blood drained from his head. It was pitch black outside anyway, so he couldn't tell if his vision had left him yet. He was quite familiar with the effects of g-induced loss of consciousness and knew the warning signs. As the ejection seat's rocket motor ran out of propellent, the force on his body subsided. Eventually, at the peak of his ejection-seat ride, the latches holding him to the seat separated and his drogue parachute deployed as the metal frame of the seat fell away in a disinterested tumble. As he soared through the night sky he took several deep breaths now that he was free of the g-forces. A few seconds later his body was jolted again as the main parachute filled and tightened the risers connecting him to the parachute.

"We hit him!" shouted the captain who had launched the ICBM at Connelly's U-2.

He could tell by the radar track which showed the target having suddenly slowed down and falling precipitously.

"Dispatch a patrol squad immediately," ordered General Seong.

Outside the facility, Sergeant Lee pointed to a six-man squad and motioned for them to get into a 2-ton truck parked outside the barracks. The men grabbed their Enfield 30-caliber bolt-action rifles and scurried into the open back of the truck. Sergeant Lee climbed into the passenger's side of the cab as a corporal started the engine and shoved the gear lever into first gear. Lee began immediately talking on the radio, trying to get information on where the pilot, should he have survived, would land.

Dozens of high-powered search lights began to crisscross the sky in search of the pilot. Captain Namgung was watching the radar track closely and had pinpointed where the bulk of the U-2 would impact the ground. He informed Sergeant Lee of where he thought the pilot might come down and the Sergeant barked directions at the truck driver.

From 20,000 feet Connelly had a spectacular view of the ICBM base and its surrounding infrastructure. His vision was periodically blinded by the flash of antiaircraft fire still rushing up from the surface by gunnery crews that had not been informed of the shoot-down. Some of the flashes were low enough and far enough away that he could actually see the U-2 as it floated mindlessly towards the ground. He felt a bit of sadness for the fantastic jet and wished it could have had a more graceful retirement. However, his grief only lasted a few seconds as his own future loomed very darkly before him. The ejection-seat style parachute offered very little maneuverability, so Connelly would land wherever the winds took him. He began to open the zippers on his space suit since he was below 10,000 feet now. He shed the pieces of the suit that he could remove and opened all the flaps and zippers. He searched inside his flightsuit and found his 9mm pistol.

Sergeant Lee, under the guidance of Captain Namgung's directions, had found the right spot. There was a searchlight on a nearby hill that had found Connelly and was tracking the pilot's descent. Lee yelled at the driver to proceed off the dirt road and into the field where the pilot would land. The driver was hesitant since he couldn't see much but knew that his superior would be unrelenting in his quest and proceeded forward. The truck bounced and shuddered as it rolled through small ditches and ran over sizable rocks. The driver was not looking up to see the pilot; rather, he did nothing besides react to the sergeant's orders. Finally, mercifully, he was given the order to stop.

Connelly looked down and could see some objects on the ground although the search light was making it hard to see much. As he got within two hundred feet of the ground he could tell that there were people and a vehicle beneath him. He was hoping that it was a farmer loading up his goods for the next day but at an altitude of one hundred feet he could see that it was a squad of Korean soldiers. For a second he considered the possibility of shooting his way through them and making for the cover of the hills, but when he saw that every man had his rifle trained on him he decided otherwise. He flung the pistol away and braced for the impact with the ground.

His feet had hardly hit the ground when the rifle butts started slamming into his ribcage. He couldn't understand all the yells and screaming but he didn't need to; there was jubilation from these soldiers getting to vent their frustration on the enemy. Apparently, the order had come down that he was to be taken alive; however, that didn't mean they couldn't beat the crap out of him. A round of kicks and blows tore most of his equipment off and his clothes began to rip under the stress. The lieutenant who was obviously in charge had ordered the truck to come over to the prisoner who was now being yanked to his feet. The old half-ton truck came to a screeching halt a few feet away and the soldiers grabbed Connelly, lifted him over their heads, and threw him into the back of the truck like a laundry bag. He put his arms out to soften the impact but he was unsure because he couldn't see in the dark and one of his eyes was swollen shut. He crashed onto the wooden flooring of the truckbed and rolled up against the steel seat rails. The soldiers piled into the back of the truck still yelling at their prize. When the lieutenant got to him he put his boot on Connelly's chest and pressed down just to make the point. Connelly had some trouble breathing but it seemed that the beating was over for now.

Two hours later he slid back into consciousness, jarred awake by the truck's unceremonious arrival at its destination. The soldiers' enthusiasm for beating him subsided due, no doubt, to the weathering effects of the bumpy truck ride. They had arrived at some sort of outpost that consisted of a main building made out of wood and canvas and a compound behind it. Once inside, Connelly was thrown into a wooden chair and secured with ropes. A well-built man entered the room and ushered the rest of the soldiers out with a flick of his hand. This guy had a well-groomed appearance accentuated by his other-worldly-smooth skin on his face. His hair was perfect and his uniform neatly pressed.

"Was Lieutenant Kim hard on you?" the man asked.

Connelly knew it was a trick question but figured he'd get beaten either way so he answered.

"No, he's pretty much a big pussy," Connelly said.

The man chuckled and then wound up a right cross and smashed Connelly in the face, knocking the chair over. After circling Connelly a couple of times, the man leaned down close to his ear.

"Yes, you're right- he is. But I am not. I am Major Gwon and you will come to know me. You will come to hate me."

Major Gwon strolled around the room for a few minutes and then left. A short time later a pair of soldiers came in, yanked Connelly up and dragged him out into the compound behind the building. It was still dark outside but the sun was beginning to rise and Connelly could make out a little bit of the terrain. There was a series of twelve small structures, six on either side of a pathway. As they dragged him down the pathway he could see that the small structures were earthen cells with rusty steel grates over the front of each one. It was hard to tell if people were in them but he sensed that at least two or three of them were currently occupied. Near the end of the pathway he was placed in front of one of the cells while one of the soldiers opened the gate and the other one tossed him in.

He hit the ground with a thud and was immediately repulsed by the stench in the cell. Apparently there was no plumbing and the cell had definitely been recently occupied. The soldiers locked the gate and then milled around the compound but seemed to be through with Connelly for a while. He let his eyes close and allowed his fatigue to carry him into a deep sleep, despite the conditions.

CHAPTER 2

The next morning he was awoken by the sound of his cell gate being opened. A soldier dropped a tray with some dirty looking rice on it and untied Connelly's hands. The soldier left and Connelly rubbed his wrists while he surveyed breakfast. It didn't look appetizing, certainly, but it didn't look lethal either and he figured this was going to be his sustenance for a while. He placed handfuls of the rice into his mouth slowly and more or less choked it down.

An hour later he was dragged out of his cell and forced to stand in a line with seven other 'residents' of the camp. Although they tried as best as they could to stand in straight lines the soldier assigned to them shouted at them and flogged them as they moved randomly, trying to appease the soldier. After a few minutes of that senseless violence they were made to march through the camp and into a room inside the main building where manacles were secured around not only their ankles but their necks. They were marched outside the building and across a small field to a dirt road which they marched down for about an hour. When they stopped, the soldier took an empty sword scabbard and smacked everyone in the head a couple of times and then beat them randomly for another minute or so. Finally, he shouted at them and pointed to a pile of shovels and picks which they moved towards and picked up. A trench, about two feet wide, twenty feet long, and three feet deep ended at their current location. Four of them went to one end of the trench while the remaining four positioned themselves at the other end. As instructed by the soldier guarding them, the group at one end began digging with their tools while the other group used their tools to refill the trench with the dirt that had just been dug out. The soldier smirked as he observed the exercise whose only point was to instill a sense of futility in the prisoners' minds.

After six hours of digging the prisoners were beaten again with the scabbard and then forced to walk back to the camp where they were crammed back into their cells. The next day, the program was repeated, the trench never gaining an inch one way or the other.

CHAPTER 3

Connelly wasn't sure what day it was anymore but it had been about two weeks since he had arrived at the prison camp. The daily labor hadn't been so bad but it did leave him exhausted at the end of the day. Even though he was used to hard work, the monotony of his situation was hard on him. To his pleasant surprise, however, it seemed like today was going to be a little different.

"Mister Johnson, you are going on a... how do you say it? 'field trip'? Is that right? Well, anyway, you're going on a ride today. I hope it hurts," Major Gwon said.

A pair of soldiers once again bound Connelly's hands behind his back and escorted him to the area in front of the main building. A weathered pickup truck was waiting there and Connelly was once again tossed into the bed. One soldier got in the back with him and another got behind the wheel. The ancient Toyota sputtered to life, belching black smoke in protest of its poor treatment over the years. The driver jammed the gearshift lever into position, grinding the gears as it lurched away from the prison camp. Connelly tried to see where they were going but the solider in the back kept Connelly positioned so that he couldn't see anything but the gunwales of the truck bed.

Every bump caused a re-ignition of the pain in his broken ribs but he was getting used to it. The ride seemed to make a number of turns and, at one point, seemed to be near the ocean since Connelly could just barely make out the scent of salt air over the pollution of the motor. The truck then ascended a very long slope that twisted up a mountainside and finally came to a halt at a landing high enough to be noticeably cooler than the prison camp.

When he was pulled out of the bed, the solider who had been in the back with him started yelling at two soldiers who were there to greet them. Even though Connelly understood basic Korean, he could not make out what they were saying due to the local dialect in their speech. He was sure, however, that his escort was warning the resident soldiers about something, presumably the value of their prisoner. There was a heated exchange and some finger pointing before they finally turned over the prisoner and left in the smoky little truck.

This outpost was indeed near the top of a fairly tall mountain. A third soldier emerged from a small wooden structure which appeared to be quarters for these isolated three. In front of the hut was a well or shaft of some kind and a depository was located behind the building.

The soldiers slapped Connelly around a little bit although it was so light that he hardly felt it. Once the smoky truck had disappeared from sight the soldiers stopped slapping him and pointed to the shaft. Connelly walked over to it and the soldier motioned for him to start turning a crank which apparently lowered a bucket of some kind down the shaft. Connelly dutifully cranked the rusty, stiff handle until the bucket clanked at the bottom of the shaft. One of the other soldiers operated some controls on the other side of the shaft that seemed to actuate some digging claws on the bucket. After a few minutes they motioned for him to bring the bucket up which he did as quickly as he could. When the bucket appeared at the mouth of the shaft one of the soldiers pulled it over and dumped its contents into a small wheel barrow and gestured for Connelly to wheel it to the depository behind the hut.

The contents of the wheel barrow seemed to be nothing more than dirt and some small stones but one of the soldiers sifted through it with moderate interest. He pulled a couple of small pieces out of the pile and slipped them in his pocket. The three talked for a minute and then motioned for Connelly to follow them around the other side of the hut which gave way to a spectacular view of the valley. The soldier who had sifted through the dirt pile sat on a stump next a small table while the other two sat at a table. Connelly sat down on the ground next to the hut and leaned back against it. None of the soldiers seemed to notice or care, which Connelly found relieving since it was almost comfortable.

The soldiers talked for a few minutes and Connelly was able to discern that the soldier who had sifted through the dirt pile was named 'Shin' and he would come to learn that the other two were 'Yong' and 'Young'. Connelly soon closed his eyes and rested his head against the wooden wall of the hut. He took a few deep breaths which felt really good in the clean air up on the mountain. He began to feel some of the bruises on his body which he had been ignoring thus far. As he relaxed, his body seemed to be taking account of itself for the first time in weeks. With his eyes closed, he used his ears to survey his surroundings. He heard the sound of birds and crickets and the gentle sound of the breeze through the nearby trees. He could hear Young and Yong playing some sort of board game, maybe dominos, and Shin was making some scraping sounds, perhaps whittling or carving. As he continued to listen, another sound crept into his consciousness, that of his heart beating. As his muscles relaxed he also began to hear the sounds of his ligaments stretching back out and his joints softly popping back into place. He savored the sounds for a while until he was interrupted by the first discordant sound he had heard since they all went behind the hut.

He opened his eyes and saw that Yong and Young were pointing fingers at each other and, after a particularly spitting retort, Young wiped the playing stones off the table and onto the ground. Connelly wasn't sure how serious this argument was but he took comfort in Shin's absolute lack of interest in what must be a common disagreement between the two game-players. After a minute of dramatic gesturing they finally came to some sort of accord and agreed to set the game back up. Feeling that the calmness was returning to the mountain retreat, he closed his eyes again.

This time he focused on his olfactory sense, letting his nose build a picture of the surroundings for him. He could smell the pine, certainly, and a waft of body odor from his hosts. There were some other subtle scents, perhaps sandalwood and the organic aroma of the debris pile decomposing. None of it was bad, especially to a man who had been locked up in the cage that Connelly was currently calling 'home'.

He was enjoying the aromatic stroll when his nose was treated to something curious and... wonderful. He searched his mental database for the identity of this sweet scent that had him relaxed and highly curious. For a moment his instinct told him to open his eyes but he resisted, savoring the challenge and the delight put on him. He tried for a few more minutes to place the scent and was just about to give up when it came to him. It was the wonderful aroma of white ginger lilies.

The second he identified the scent, his shoulders slid down into a very relaxed position and the wrinkles on his forehead subsided. He breathed in deeply, reveling in the delicious sensation. Since the shoot-down and subsequent beating, his mind had been loathe to concentrate too hard on anything. At this point he was living in the ephemeral joy of ginger lilies but his mind started to work on a slightly deeper level again. After a few more minutes of increasing thoughtfulness, the ridges began to return to his forehead as he asked himself where the scent was coming from. He continued to keep his eyes closed tightly in a game he was playing with his own mind- the temptation to open them was great and the challenge delighted him.

He continued to search his thoughts for a source of the lovely scent but was sure that white ginger lilies did not grow in this part of the world at this elevation. It baffled him. Then, in a sudden rush of pleasure, he remembered where the powerful scent lived in his memory: Lauren. He recalled the night in Philadelphia when he told her how much the scent of her perfume turned him on and she, in turn, explained that it was a rare perfume based on the white ginger lily and how that flower is native to the Himalayas. She went on to describe the flower's preference for wet, well-drained soils and was about to describe its widespread cultivation in tropical Asia when Connelly interrupted her by kissing her hard on the lips.

For a second his mind entertained the impossible thought that Lauren was nearby and the scent of her perfume was wafting to Connelly as a secret signal to him. The total impossibility of that forced his eyelids open and he saw her standing in front of him. The shadowy silhouette of a beautiful woman stood strongly but elegantly before him. He strained to focus on her and groaned as the image metamorphosed into an intricate pattern of light and dark in Shin's clothes and the woods behind him. At hearing Connelly's groan, Shin looked over casually and then returned his focus to his carving.

Connelly slumped again, knowing that this hallucination was his mind's way of protesting his predicament and trying to soothe him. It concerned him, since it had only been a few weeks and he wondered what this meant for the coming weeks and maybe months or years of his incarceration.

He slumped back against the wooden hut wall and dozed in and out of consciousness for several hours until he was slapped on the shoulder by Yong. Connelly immediately got up and followed the three to the front of the hut where the well was located. He heard the sound of the little Toyota truck straining its way up the hill and realized Young was directing him to operate the crank. Connelly quickly started turning the crank, not wanting to pay any disrespect to the slack that these guys were giving him.

When the Toyota came to a whiny halt, the soldier jumped out of the back of the truck and approached with his rifle in hand. Yong started yelling at Connelly and suddenly spun him around. Young closed in tightly and slapped Connelly across the face. Shin skipped over and, putting his foot on top of Connelly's foot, pushed him so that he fell on the ground. Connelly let out an exaggerated groan worthy of a good stomach punch or two and curled up on the ground. The soldier from the truck seemed pleased and dragged Connelly across the ground and kicked him as he climbed into the truck but otherwise left him alone. The ride back down the mountain to the prison camp was rough and each bump in the road sent shockwaves through Connelly's body. They finally reached the camp and Connelly was thrown back into his cage. He wondered if he would ever get to return to the mountain retreat.

CHAPTER 4

General Arristol sat down at Jurgensen's desk without any invitation.

"So, where is Connelly?" the general asked.

Jurgensen slid back from his desk and put his hands in his lap.

"I don't know," was the reply.

"Dammit, Mack, what happened to him?" the general asked.

"I guess he screwed up," Jurgensen said.

"I doubt that. Anyway, what's the status of the investigation?"

"The Navy hasn't found any wreckage at sea and satellite overflights haven't revealed anything," Jurgensen said. "The media is reporting that several missiles, including a Taepodong-2, were fired out of the No-dong launch facility, designed to scare Japan and the U.S."

"Was that your bit of fiction?" Arristol asked.

"Yes, mostly," Jurgensen replied with a proud grin on his face.

"Well, that's a real extensive effort you've put forward," Arristol sarcastically replied.

"The NSA doesn't want to make a big deal out of this for political reasons and Pyongyang hasn't sent any postcards," Jurgensen offered tersely, his grin turning to a scowl immediately.

"Well, that's just great," General Arristol said, adding, under his breath, "You bastard..."

CHAPTER 5

Connelly had gotten back into his routine of carving a miniature latrine trench in his cage that was swept away each day by the guards. They always yelled at him and shook their fingers at him but didn't seem inclined to punish him more than that. It seemed that they took delight in destroying what he created each day but they didn't realize that Connelly took just as much delight in making them do something they didn't want to do every day.

Connelly didn't know it, but it was Tuesday again. He thought he heard the sound of the beat-up little Toyota, a suspicion confirmed when he was dragged out of his cage and beat up on the way to the front of the compound. He had become accustomed to the beatings although he was sure his ribs were grossly disfigured beneath his bruised skin. They threw him on the ground next to the pickup truck where the soldier from the week before hopped out, kicked him a few times, and then threw him into the back of the truck for the bumpy ride up the mountain.

He had guessed how long the ride would take, based on last week's trip, and tried to count the number of seconds until he got there. He was at 1,546 when the truck screeched to a halt and the soldier dumped him off the tailgate. He yelled to the driver to speed away which resulted in a ghastly cloud of black smoke being belched into his face and a stream of pebbles and twigs thrown onto him. He could hear the soldier laugh as the truck rumbled away.

Young, Yong, and Shin stood Connelly up and pointed to the well which Connelly walked over to and began cranking. When the bucket came up Shin once again sifted through the contents and pulled a small stone out. Young and Yong went around the back of the hut to resume their mahjong game and Shin watched as Connelly dumped the dirt onto the compost pile. They walked together to the back of the hut and Shin pointed to the ground where Connelly had sat last week. Connelly dutifully and thankfully sat down, brushing the twigs and pebbles off of himself as Shin sat back on his stool and began carving. Connelly watched for a minute, trying to see what exactly Shin was doing but it was difficult from his vantage point. Connelly eventually gave up and looked out over the valley. It was a beautiful day and he could see for miles. He dozed off for a while and once again was awoken by Yong and Young arguing about their game. The disagreement was resolved more quickly this time and the two returned to their game without spilling the pieces on the ground.

Connelly rested his head and closed his eyes, breathing deeply. It took a while but he found the ethereal scent of ginger lilies again. Lauren immediately jumped into his consciousness, her shoulder-length brown hair resting softly on her shoulders. In his mind the image was becoming clear and he could see that she was standing in a green field. He wanted to rush towards her but he knew that might end the fantasy. He had enough conscious control to restrain his dreams and forced himself to take it slowly. He concentrated on her again and then tried to discern where she was. It took a few minutes but he recognized the surroundings- it was a park in Washington D.C. with booths and tents all around. He picked up the smell of grilled food with heavy seasoning and realized that it was the Korean Arts Festival where he had first met Lauren so many years ago.

"Lauren, this is Midshipman Connelly- he's in my foreign policy class," Doctor Carano told her daughter.

"It's nice to meet you," Lauren offered politely.

"It's my pleasure," Connelly returned.

Connelly had accompanied his foreign policy professor to this festival since he had really come to admire and like Doctor

Carano. She was a guest lecturer at the Naval Academy and was well-liked in general for her piercing analysis of foreign policy, past and present. She sometimes came off as gruff but Connelly had learned to appreciate her directness and he learned a lot from her analytical style. She had told Connelly that her daughter would be meeting them at the festival but the fact that her daughter was about Connelly's age was a pleasant surprise. He was immediately taken with her graceful gate and charming looks and had to force himself to retard his advances towards her. Connelly figured it was likely that she got hit on by most of Carano's students.

They spent a couple of hours at the festival, tasting the food and discussing the overall style of the Korean art displayed at the festival. As they left the park and walked to the subway station, Connelly caught a scent that had been overwhelmed by the spice in the food at the festival. It was the alluring scent of fragrant flowers that subtly accompanied Lauren. Connelly had never really cared for perfume, mostly because the girls in high school had put on way too much. The choice in scents and the perfect application of it spun some wheels in Connelly. He was already thirsting for more contact with her. They said their goodbyes and Connelly ached a bit at the thought of not seeing her again. It would be difficult but he was determined to see her again.

Lauren left Connelly and his eyes opened to see Shin studiously working on his carving. Young and Yong were engrossed in their game so Connelly turned his attention to Shin. For the first time Shin had turned slightly towards Connelly and held his carving pieces between his knees as he worked. This afforded Connelly an excellent view of what the Korean man was doing and Connelly was intrigued. The man had a piece of jade about four inches long in one hand and a rat tail file in the other. His strokes were quick but careful. The file was pretty dull, no doubt from years of use, and, as a result, individual strokes didn't have a significant effect on the piece. It worked out though, since Shin obviously had no pressure to finish this piece anytime in the next few years. The care he demonstrated showed his delight in the craft and his deft touch revealed years of practice. Connelly stared intently at the piece and watched carefully as the man slid the file over one spot three times then quickly moved to another spot and worked the groove there with four strokes. The pattern changed and Connelly could see slow progress being made. At this point it wasn't clear what the final product would be but Connelly was fascinated by the hobby which he had never known anything about. After fifteen minutes Shin returned the piece to the tabletop, took a break to rest his hand, and continued carving. Connelly could no longer see the piece but had committed a detailed image of it in his mind.

A few hours later the Toyota sputtered up the mountainside and the abuse parade was conducted again. On the bumpy ride back to the camp he concentrated on the image he had stored in his mind of the artwork that Shin was creating. It was fascinating to Connelly.

The following week Connelly was taken up the mountainside and made to work the winch as usual. After they all settled in behind the wooden hut Connelly drifted off as usual. In his mind he saw the trees on the mountainside with birds fluttering about and the sound of the wind softly washing through the limbs. He saw himself walking down the side of the mountain, his pace increasing with each step. He looked up at one point and saw the Washington Memorial. His body returned to a healthy physique and he stepped easily onto the lawn in the Mall lined by the Smithsonians. There were people around him, mostly tourists, gabbing about the wonders in the museums and trying to find their places on picture maps. Connelly was startled slightly when the soft, warm skin of Lauren's hand slipped into his. As she sidled closer to him he picked up that wonderful scent of her perfume and he could feel the lively bounce in her step as their intertwined hands swung forward and back. Lauren loved the Museum of Natural History and had no problem pulling Connelly through the doors with her. The gentle click-clack of her high heels tapping on the marble floor created a cadence that showcased her feminine appeal and Connelly was hooked on the rhythm. They went through the various chambers with Connelly listening as Lauren described the exhibits with almost expert knowledge.

"AJ, did you know that dinosaurs were in Kansas? Recently, a *Liodon Dyspelor* fossil was found near Smokey Hill River. Isn't that incredible?" Lauren asked rhetorically.

"Yes, that is amazing," Connelly replied.

As she described the paleontology exhibit, he found it difficult to concentrate as he almost stared at her beautiful lips. She was wearing, on this occasion, a light lip gloss that added a touch of color and just enough shine to make her lips luscious and inviting. He could feel the attraction pulling at him but he resisted any advances on her, not wanting to screw up something potentially wonderful by being too aggressive. In most of the classes at the Academy he was being trained to be aggressive and assertive and, ironically, that emphasis made him more cautious than usual in this situation. As they moved on to the next exhibit showcase the enticing click-clack of her heels gave way to a less precise sound, more of a sliding sound. Connelly felt Lauren moving ahead of him more quickly as he was, inexplicably, unable to keep up with her. The strain on his grip of her hand increased and the sliding sound became louder until it was a grinding sound. He snapped his eyes open and saw Shin working a large piece of sandstone with a flat file.

For the next three weeks Connelly continued to have dreams and fantasies about Lauren coming to see him on the mountain and their spending time together in Washington. Whenever he awoke, Connelly saw Shin working his file on a piece of stone, each one taking shape slowly as the sound of a file grinding on stone mixed with the inebriated Yong and Young's constant arguing.

The next time he visited the so-called work station, he took his usual seat against the wooden hut and watched Shin work the piece of jade. As Connelly's eyelids slid shut, his mind took him down the mountain and across the ocean to Washington and Lauren. They had enjoyed a wonderful meal of Kurobuta pork chops and Maine diver scallops at the 1789 Restaurant in Georgetown and had made their way down to the C&O Canal.

The spotless white fabric of Connelly's uniform, with its crisp black trim, blended beautifully with Lauren's halter-top dress. The dress was mostly black with gold swaths of color following the seams running down the sides of her torso emptying into the flaring of the skirt. Connelly was mesmerized by the way the dress clung tightly at the top and rustled about at the bottom when she walked. Her dark brown hair waved lazily in the light breeze and the evening sunlight lit her face like a portrait. He was hazy with attraction and desire. They didn't say much as they walked along, both content and joyous in each other's company, which was good since Connelly couldn't have concentrated enough to participate in a meaningful discussion of any kind.

When they got to the end of the pier they stood close to one another and watched the cargo ships in the distance make their approach to Washington Harbor. They had both been to this place before but this was a new experience for both of them- to feel the wonderful fire that flows through every inch of the body when desire peaks. Connelly put his hand on Lauren's back and gently caressed the incredibly smooth skin of her back. He could feel the shape of her back, the smooth edges of her toned muscles and the delightful paths his fingertips took cresting the ridge of her shoulder blade.

With each pass back and forth, his pulse quickened and she felt her legs begin to tremble. Simultaneously they turned towards each other and his eyes fell into her deep, dark, sultry brown eyes. She looked up into his sharp, clear blue eyes and square jaw and sensed a delicious mix of strength and gentleness in him. With his right hand around the small of her back pulling them together, he raised his left hand and touched her cheek as gently as a lightning bug. Not wanting to disturb such a beautiful creation, his fingertips gently grazed over her cheek and along the line of her chin and then back up into the hair behind her ear. She had wrapped her arms around his waist and held him tight against her, her fingers digging into his back with the strength of her passion.

The desire welled up in him and overtook him with hurricane-like force. He thrust his lips against her luscious, dark red lips and his hand slid around through her hair to the back of her head, holding their lips tight. Their embrace tightened, welded by passion and powered by the fury of their kisses.

Suddenly a piling shot out of the water and struck Connelly in the head, knocking him to the ground. He opened his eyes to see Yong punching Young in the head. Apparently, the game of mahjong had gone bad, again, and Yong hit Young with his flask and then jumped over the table to pummel him. In the ensuing brawl Yong had kicked Connelly in the head and then fell on him as they rolled around punching and kicking one another.

As Connelly rubbed his left temple he felt the slight trickle of blood resulting from the crash. He looked up to see Shin still working his piece of jade, immune to the brawl. He did, however, intervene when the drunken belligerents approached the edge of the cliff. Shin put down his file and jade stone and grabbed the men, one in each hand, by grasping a handful of skin on each man's chest. Clearly the stone carving had developed very powerful hands and the fighters knew that

Shin was not to be messed with. They quickly desisted with their scuffle and, brushing off their tunics, picked up the game pieces and reset the table.

Shin shot them each an annoyed glance and then walked slowly over to Connelly. He looked at the wound and went inside the hut, returning with a small cloth. He marched over to the game table and took Young's flask without saying a word. He moistened the cloth with alcohol from the flask and rubbed the wound on Connelly's head. The alcohol stung a little but Connelly didn't even flinch.

When he finished, Connelly did his best to apply the right accent when he said, "Kamsahamnida", thanking Shin in his native tongue. Shin was surprised to hear the American speak at all, much less in Korean. He responded with a quick nod and tossed the flask back to Young, then he returned to his carving.

CHAPTER 6

The next week Connelly picked up his daydream where he had left off previously, recalling the wonderful evening that ensued after Lauren and Connelly's first kiss on the pier. That night of unmitigated passion and desire had been burned into his memory like a stone engraving. Those were the most pleasant memories he had and it felt good to relive them so realistically. He felt a tinge in his heart for his feelings towards Lauren, knowing that wherever she was today, he would not see her. Nor would he tomorrow, but in this existence tomorrow was a concept too abstract to waste his time with. The power of the moment only served to heighten his re-found time with Lauren and it made him calm and content.

When he opened his eyes this time, Shin was glancing over at him. Noticing that he had come out of his predictable trance, Shin stood up and walked over to Connelly. As the Korean man looked down at Connelly it seemed that he was considering something deeply. He finally relaxed the muscles in his face, apparently deciding the decision wasn't so important after all. He then tossed a piece of sandstone onto the ground next to Connelly and followed by handing him a well-worn rat tail file. He watched to see Connelly's reaction and was pleased when the prisoner eagerly picked up the 'art supplies'. Connelly bowed his head and once again said 'thank you' in Korean. Satisfied, Shin returned to his work table and resumed carving the piece of jade he had been working on for weeks, its shape now clearly a prowling tiger.

Connelly was overcome with delight at the prospect of carving something other than a latrine trench into the floor of his cage back at the camp. The trust Shin had shown him was considerable and Connelly felt honored by it. He was also earnestly interested in this art of stone carving. He didn't know the first thing about it beyond what he had garnered by watching his captor's delicate and persistent strokes.

Connelly took the file and gripped it with his calloused, swollen fingers. He hadn't done any delicate detailed work since his imprisonment. When he was flying the U-2 his fingers had developed a stunning agility since the Dragon Lady required an expert touch in many phases of its flight regime. Now he struggled to grasp the file with any sort of dexterity, but he managed and began dragging it across the piece of stone. At first his strokes merely bobbled across the surface of the stone and then, when he pressed harder, jumped and skipped as the file dug in and released repeatedly. He was concentrating so hard on the task that he had pulled the stone within four or five inches of his face. He hadn't looked at anything in detail in the months he had been imprisoned so it was an extra treat to concentrate on details once again. For the first twenty minutes he struggled to make smooth draws on the stone, resulting in more than one jab into his fingers with the pointy end of the file. On the rare occasions that the file missed his calluses, a prick of blood sprouted on his fingers, but he hardly noticed or cared except that it began to stain the beautiful, light color of the sandstone. He rubbed his fingers on his tunic to wipe the blood away and then continued drawing the dull file across the piece of stone.

Two hours after he had started, it was time to quit since the little yellow Toyota could be heard struggling up the mountain road. Shin pointed down the mountain at the truck and Connelly immediately responded by handing the stone and , more importantly, the file back to Shin. He again bowed and thanked the man. Although Shin responded with a casual wave of his hand, he felt a little better inside, knowing that he was sharing something he cared about. They both quietly looked forward to the next week.

For the next three weeks Connelly continued working on his carving, developing a feel for how the steel file rubbed the stone. He would become engrossed for long stretches of time and hated having to return the pieces and go back down the mountain.

One particularly cold Tuesday, Connelly was getting worried when the usual time for him to be taken to the mountain camp came and went without any explanation. Several hours later Major Gwon appeared, strolling down the main pathway running between the cells. He stopped in front of Connelly's cage and bent down to look at him.

"How are you today, Mister Johnson?"

"Great! I had a tremendous bowel movement this morning- it's right over there, if you're hungry," he replied.

Gwon smiled broadly, then motioned for the guards to pull him out of the cage. Connelly stood limply and waited as the Korean tyrant wound up a right cross and knocked Connelly to the ground. He followed with a kick to the ribs and dug a heel into Connelly's cheek to finish off the exercise.

The guards dragged him back into his cage and secured it as Gwon strolled away towards the cells near the back of the camp. Once the ringing in his ears stopped, Connelly could hear Gwon yelling to the guards to pull various prisoners out of their cages. He assembled six of them on the main avenue, including two young females. They were all dirty, beaten, and hungry just like Connelly. Gwon lined them up into two files and marched them into the main building. Connelly never saw them again.

CHAPTER 7

On Tuesday of the following week Connelly heard the little Toyota sputter as it pulled into the camp. The sound of that creaky, smokey little rust bucket had come to be music to Connelly's ears. He actually had to hide his enthusiasm at the thought of leaving the camp for a few hours and getting to work on his stone carving.

He heard the bellicose soldier approach his cell as usual but was shocked when Gwon appeared. The guards pulled Connelly from the cell and the pungent smell of whiskey hit him immediately.

"Mister Johnson," he slurred. "I am going to take you to the mountain camp today! Won't that be great? Aren't you honored?"

"Great," was all Connelly could muster, not knowing what lay in store for him and the implications of this change.

Gwon pulled a whiskey bottle out of his back pocket and showed it to Connelly, who didn't move. Gwon, teetering for a second, then swung the bottle at Connelly's face, producing a resounding 'pop' when it struck his cheek.

As the guards escorted Connelly to the main building and into the truck, he could feel the blood pooling in his mouth and he decided to let it trickle down his chin so that Gwon might be happy and not decide to smash the bottle across his head. True to his word, Gwon hopped into the back of the truck with him and they sputtered down the road towards the mountain camp.

Gwon had been singing old Korean songs, taking swigs of whiskey in between verses. Since Gwon was about half-gone anyway, Connelly took a chance and sat up on the floor of the truckbed. Gwon didn't seem to notice or care and Connelly salivated at the opportunity to look around. About half way to the camp they passed slowly through a small village, explaining something Connelly had wondered about on each trip up the mountain. He looked around, surveying the huts and other small buildings. It seemed like a small farming village with a few people milling about. Most people stared at him since it was quite unusual to see a caucasian in this part of the world. He dismissed the stares but was intrigued by one particular man and a woman who seemed to be looking not at him but at Gwon and the truck. Surely they had seen the truck every Tuesday for the last six months, so what were they looking at?

After they passed through the farming village, the road steepened and the weak little truck struggled to climb the mountain. Gwon continued downing his whiskey at an impressive rate and had emptied the bottle as they arrived at the camp.

Young, Yong, and Shin met Gwon at the truck, looking a little surprised and anxious. Gwon stumbled out of the back of the truck and staggered for a few seconds. Connelly let himself out of the truck to save everyone the misery of Gwon trying to do it. When the drunk bastard realized where he was and the his prisoner was there with him, he impulsively smashed the base of the whiskey bottle on the fender of the truck, producing a bottle with sharp, jagged edges on it. Gripping it by the neck, he swung at Connelly, who stood still, and missed. Infuriated, he lunged at Connelly and raked the bottle across his shoulder and chest.

Although it seemed that he was aiming for Connelly's neck or head, the sight of the blood running down his chest and arms seemed sufficient for the sadistic bastard and he stumbled back to the truck. With his feet still on the ground, he slumped his torso onto the tailgate and laid his head down onto the cold, dirty metal and passed out. The driver and the other guard who came from the camp looked at each other and then at Connelly. The prisoner walked over and grabbed Gwon's feet and tossed them unceremoniously into the truck bed. The driver instinctively reached for his pistol but didn't pull it out of its holster. He instead grunted disapprovingly at Connelly and then hopped back into the truck. The other guard got in and they rumbled away, the sound of Gwon's body bouncing around in the bed of truck providing some comedy that no one laughed about out loud.

Shin motioned for Connelly to forego the ritual well dig and led him into the hut while Yong and Young settled into their perpetual game of mahjong. Shin had Connelly sit in a chair while he wiped the blood with a somewhat clean towel. He dabbed some alcohol on the cloth and wiped the cuts briefly then he took Connelly outside where he sat in his usual place against the wall of the hut.

Immediately Connelly closed his eyes and his mind drifted away. He and Lauren were returning to their hotel in Bangkok or Singapore or wherever they were on this imaginary date. As they entered the room, he followed her and savored the sight of her trim figure filling the curves of her sensuous black and white striped dress. The handkerchief hemline rose above her right knee and the silky material swished back and forth with each step. Even with three-inch heels she walked confidently and gracefully and almost bounced across the room and out onto the balcony. Connelly followed her and wrapped his arms around her from behind as they looked out over the harbor on that warm September evening. He put his chin near her ear and felt her hair tickle his neck as she reached back and ran her fingers through his short hair.

Despite all the energy surging through him, Connelly began to feel very sleepy. He struggled to keep his eyes open but couldn't stop them and soon his head was resting comfortably on her shoulder. He could still smell her sweet perfume and hear the sounds of the small motor boats below but he couldn't open his eyes. He felt a little unsteady and grasped her tighter to steady himself. It seemed that the ground beneath him began to tilt and he reached out with one arm to grab onto something but couldn't see anything in the pitch darkness behind his eyelids. He fell and smashed his head on one of the wooden chairs on the balcony.

When he opened his eyes, Shin was looking to see how badly he hurt himself when he fell over. His head hitting the hard ground sounded like a coconut falling from a tree but he didn't seem to be bleeding or unconscious so Shin went back to his carving. Connelly groaned as he righted himself and wiped the spittle that had run down his cheek when he was asleep. The slimy combination of spit and blood quickly brought him back to the present. He rubbed his face a few times and took a few deep breaths to clear his lungs. The breaths stretched his chest and the fresh lacerations stung with disapproval. He slumped back down and sat quietly for the rest of the day.

CHAPTER 8

Two weeks later, Connelly's normal Tuesday trip up the mountain was pre-empted by another one of Gwon's drunken beatings and escort up the mountain. The following week the pattern returned to normal. Connelly became accustomed to this life, taking great emotional refuge in the Tuesday carving sessions and the wonderful replays of his relationship with Lauren playing out almost in real-time. His body deteriorated to a point of equilibrium in which he weighed sixty pounds less than his pre-imprisonment weight of one-hundred-ninety pounds. For a six-foot tall man, one-hundred-thirty pounds looks like a worn leather cape strung over the tops of pointy furniture posts. His face had sunken in, all the minute traces of fat long-ago metabolized and his eyes looking prominent in his skull. Nevertheless, after six months his body had adjusted and he was staying alive on his meager food rations and his immune system continued to fight off the threat of infection posed by frequent lacerations and his unsanitary accommodations. The weekly trip to see Shin and work on his carvings was enough to keep him alive for the twenty-one months since he had been captured. But things were about to change on his next trip up the mountain on a gorgeous spring day in early June.

CHAPTER 9

The little Toyota dutifully made its way up the mountain again. Three months prior to this trip Connelly had tried sitting up in the bed of the truck and found that the guard had either been given new, relaxed rules or simply had tired of beating him down. He had enjoyed the spectacular view of the mountainside and the ocean below. On the last couple of trips up the mountain he had noticed the same curious couple in the farming village watching them closely as they passed by. The other residents had become accustomed to seeing Connelly in the truck and had long since become inured to his appearance, but not these two.

After the ritual slapping around and subsequent charade, Connelly took his spot on the ground next to the wooden hut. He had, by this time, worn a spot on the ground which was decorated with the green, tan, and gray powder resulting from his more than a year of carving. Shin had given him a new file several months ago which was necessitated by Connelly's having completely worn the teeth off of the first one. Shin had come to appreciate Connelly's interest in the art and even kind of liked him and admired how quickly he learned stone carving. In recognition he had given Connelly a piece of jade about four inches long and two inches in diameter, quite a treasure under any circumstance but especially this one. Connelly did what he could to thank the reluctant guard but his resources were limited and thus it usually amounted to helping clean up around the hut and picking up Yong and Young's playing pieces after their habitual fights.

Connelly was touched by the gift of the jade blank and took great care to carve it carefully. He had spent an entire day just deciding what to carve and finally decided that this very special piece of jade required a subject worthy of its beauty and value and thus he chose to carve a likeness of Lauren. Carving a human figure is quite a challenge since the human eye is very critical of its likeness, but Connelly was determined to capture in stone what his heart and mind had lived on every day.

Over the weeks he had shaved tiny grains of jade off the blank and slowly the human form took shape. The gently waves of Lauren's hair became apparent in the upper end of the blank and her long, sleek legs were the focus of the lower half. Capturing the slopes of her back and the curves of her breasts came surprisingly easily to Connelly but depicting her face was daunting. Finally, seeing his trouble, Shin showed him some of his other carving and demonstrated techniques for rendering the human expression. Even though he had no idea what Lauren looked like, it was apparent that he had seen enough American girls and was quite helpful in showing Connelly how to capture the features properly.

One particularly pleasant day, he finished the rendering of her and he sat for an hour staring at the amateur rendering of his memory. He was very pleased with the figurine's ability to stir positive energy in him and he became agitated when he saw how low the sun was on the horizon, knowing that with it came the little Toyota. He found great peace and hope in the figurine and wanted to keep it with him.

As the truck made its final turn for the drive up the steep hill, Connelly walked over to Shin and showed him the finished piece. Shin smiled with approval and nodded a few times. Connelly then took a short breath and glanced at Yong and Young. Confident they weren't looking, he showed Shin a small pocket that he had formed in his tunic, made by folding the fabric over and tying the rope around his waist in just the right way. Shin understood and, when Connelly motioned that he wanted to put the figurine in his pocket, Shin glanced at the other two, grabbed the figurine, and stuffed it into Connelly's pocket and walked away quickly.

The guard from the truck didn't slap him around too hard this time and the figurine stayed securely in Connelly's makeshift pocket as they got in the truck and headed down the mountain. Every five minutes or so he would very discreetly rub his arm across abdomen to make sure the figurine was still there; to lose it at this point would be heartbreaking.

As they approached the farming village Connelly could, once again, see the ocean off to his left. He gazed at it in the fading light and wondered if he would ever get close to it again. When they entered the village, the truck slowed as it always did and the usual villagers ignored them. As they rounded the last turn Connelly's eyes caught the overly-inquisitive couple and, an instant later, a thunderous roar shot up from under the truck! The feeble little Toyota flipped onto its side and began to slide off the road. Connelly grasped the railing in the truck bed and squeezed with all the might he could muster. The guard, who had been sitting on the bench seat in the bed of the truck, was immediately thrown when the truck flipped up on its side. Connelly never saw him again.

As the truck slid on the dirt and rocks he could hear the driver and other guard screaming. A few seconds went by and they were now slipping off the road and heading down the hillside. Connelly could see trees whipping past as the truck gained speed and the crunching sound of rocks beating up the truck body. The truck flipped back and forth, spinning around at the mercy of the various immovable objects it struck. At one point the truck had almost stopped so Connelly took the opportunity to leap from the bed of the truck. He had no idea where this leap of faith would take him but it was worth trying. He tumbled on the ground and spun harmlessly to a stop a few seconds later. When he had regained his senses he looked up to see the truck upside-down, wedged into a rock crevice. The gas tank and fuel lines had been severely torn up and gas had poured all over the truck. Any one of a number of sparks could have taken credit for setting the mess ablaze and it really didn't matter now which one had done it. Connelly looked, stunned, as the fire whipped itself into an inferno. He couldn't tell what had happened to the driver but the other guard had scrambled from the vehicle with only a few seconds to spare.

When the fire had melted through the radiator hose, the poor little truck vomited the greenish-orange fluid violently onto the ground; when the fire burned the insulation off of the wires under the hood the headlights flashed on and off wildly and the horn surrendered the last gasps of life as the truck thrashed in its death throes. Connelly felt a bit of mourning for the little truck since it had become one of only two steady companions here that hadn't abused him.

He was snapped out of his gaze by the sound of the mysterious man and woman from the village running down the hillside towards him. Connelly got to his feet and slipped out of sight in a small culvert. He watched as the couple approached, expecting them to help their comrade who had escaped the blaze. He saw the man jog over to the guard and extend his arm to help the man up. To his total shock and amazement he stared, open-jawed, as the man squeezed the trigger on the small pistol in his hand, the shot instantly killing the guard. The man ran back over to the woman who was holding a bundle of blankets. They talked excitedly, gesturing at the truck and pointing down the hillside. The woman had some trouble gesturing and Connelly quickly realized why when he saw the tiny face of a baby in the woman's arms, wrapped in the blanket. Although he had learned a lot of Korean during his imprisonment, he could not understand their dialect but it was clear that they had caused the truck to leave the road, perhaps by the use of a small explosive. With their getaway plan now burning only a few feet away, they were clearly panicking. Finally, the man gestured down the hill and began running with the woman quick on his heels.

Connelly did not know what to do; his instinct was to make his way back up the hill to Shin but he quickly dismissed the idea, figuring that the other two guards would undoubtedly blame the wreck and dead guards on Connelly. He saw only one other option and he took it- he ran after the couple down the hill.

CHAPTER 10

At first it was difficult to keep up with them since the light was beginning to fade. However, with there being three of them, Connelly was able to close the distance eventually. He was surprised at his speed and agility given that he had spent the last twenty-one months doing little more than stretching for exercise. The days of hard labor kept his muscles somewhat toned but the poor diet prevented any accumulation of muscle mass and the nature of the work did not provide cardiovascular health. Nevertheless, the adrenaline in his system powered him forward, hopping over tree stumps and traversing ditches as he raced down the hillside in pursuit of the mystery couple.

After ten minutes or so he closed within twenty-five yards of the couple and they stopped upon hearing his footsteps in the brush. They carefully searched through the woods, looking for Connelly who had stopped cold in his tracks. After a few seconds they saw him and exchanged a few words with one another, undoubtedly assessing the risk he posed and how they should respond. They didn't ponder long, however, and resumed their speedy trek down the mountainside, occasionally glancing back at the strange American following them.

As he pursued the fleeing family, Connelly felt his feet start to hurt and realized that the various rocks and sharp sticks had cut into his bare feet. The thick calluses he had developed protected the bottoms of his feet but the sides and top were being lacerated constantly and the blood began to paint his feet red. Despite the irritation, he continued at flank speed and closed to within ten yards of the family. The father looked back at him for only a second and then helped his wife up a large step and then followed himself. Connelly struggled a little as the wedges in the rock dug into the sides of his feet but he kept going.

Another twenty minutes of scurrying brought the family to the front side of a very steep and rather tall rock face. The mother secured the baby in a sack on her back and the father helped push them up the rock face. He grabbed her foot and lifted, steadied her when she began to tilt, and then grunted when he propelled her up the final foot of the climb at which point she grabbed the lip at the top of the rock face and pulled herself and the baby up.

Connelly stood a few yards away, patiently watching as the family struggled to escape up the rock face. The mother tried to reach down and help the man but she couldn't reach far enough to help. He struggled to get a foothold but his leather moccasins slipped on the smooth surface. Connelly looked nearby and realized that the only way forward required ascending the rock face. He did notice, however, that a different route up the rock a few yards away showed promise. He stepped up to the rock and began climbing. His fingers cringed and popped as he put his weight onto their joints and he found his arms to be a mere shadow of the powerful limbs they were two years ago. The muscles in his stomach twisted and cramped under the sudden exertion and on several occasions he thought of letting go and collapsing to the ground. But he persevered and made it up to the top of the outcropping and stood only a few feet away from the mother and her baby.

The woman cowered and shuffled back a few feet, cradling her baby deep in her arms. Her brow furled, she looked almost animalistic in her instinctive defensive posture. She glanced down at her husband who was pointing a finger at Connelly in a powerless gesture. He shouted a few things that Connelly did not understand and looked from the man to the woman and back.

In a careful gesture, he pointed to an extra blanket the woman had wrapped around her waist. At first she was frightened and confused but eventually unwrapped the blanket and threw it to him in a gesture of appeasement. She hoped he would go away.

Connelly knelt down and laid the blanket out flat. He then rolled it tightly, going from one corner to the diagonal opposite, producing a six-foot long rather sturdy length of improvised cord. He took one of the remaining corners and tied a knot around the cord so that it would not unravel. He then dug his left hand into a crevice at the edge of the rock and clamped his hand down as firmly as he could. He lowered the blanket-cord down with his right hand and, with the addition of his six-foot or so wingspan the six-foot long blanket-cord reached low enough for the man to grasp.

The older Korean man licked his lips and squinted at Connelly in a moment of serious judgment. Only a moment passed, though, and the man took hold of the blanket and pulled himself upwards. The strain on Connelly's body was tremendous and he let out several loud grunts as the man's weight was partially carried by Connelly's weakened muscles and ligaments. When the man reached the top of the blanket he grabbed Connelly's forearm with both his hands and squeezed so hard Connelly thought his bones might be crushed. He let go of the blanket and grasped his hand around the man's arm and counted in English, hoping the Korean man would understand.

"One, two , three!" Connelly shouted and pulled upwards with all the might he had left.

At the same moment the man pushed upwards with his toes and pulled as hard as he could and the combined force launched him high enough that he was able to scramble onto the top of the rock face and embrace his wife.

Connelly rolled over and lay on his back, out of breath with his muscles burning from the strain. He closed his eyes for a few seconds. When he opened them again the Korean man was leaning towards him and looking intently. Satisfied that he was alive, the man continued on with his wife.

The exhaustion overwhelmed Connelly and the desire to lay still on the cool rock was great. He realized quickly that if he stayed there it would be his eternal resting place and forced himself back to his feet. With a couple of deep breaths he launched himself in the direction the family had gone and after a few minutes he caught up with them.

CHAPTER 11

An hour later the ad-hoc family moved in a group. It was dark now and the going was very slow. If not for the bright moonlight their progress would have been completely halted over the foreboding terrain. Connelly could hear the ocean and after two more hours of difficult walking they found themselves on the beach. As the family rested at the top of the beach Connelly took the opportunity to walk across the sand.

The salt water stung his open wounds a little bit but he knew it would help wash them and the water felt so good. The sand oozed through his toes and the sensation was amazing. He bent down and ran his hands through it like a child, enjoying every sensation and rubbing it on his hands. The sand and the water exfoliated almost two years' worth of dead skin, stripping away dirt and debris. Eventually, he turned away and sat with the family for a few minutes. The couple talked in a hushed voice and occasionally said something to Connelly. The only word he could understand was 'boat' and he hoped it meant that a boat was coming for them. Unfortunately he did not understand anything else and had to wait for the events to unfold before he found out.

CHAPTER 12

Several hours later the first wisps of light wafted above the horizon. The Korean couple got to their feet, the father stretching and the mother tending to their baby which had stayed remarkably quiet the last few hours. The father took several steps towards the water and looked down the beach to the south. He squinted as he looked for something in the morning darkness and apparently found it as he then gestured to his wife to join him. Connelly instinctively followed and the four of them made their way down the beachfront. The man was diligently surveying the ridge line above them and made several gestures to Connelly, quietly admonishing him to make as little noise as possible- no doubt the Korean Army was looking for the runaway group.

A few minutes later Connelly saw what the man had seen down the beach- a cargo ship that was tied up at the end of a pier. At first Connelly didn't think too much about the ship but then, as he considered the scene, realized that something wasn't right. The ship was dark- no running lights, search lights, or overhead lights on the bridge or anywhere else. The only light coming from the ship was a dull yellow glow seeping out of the open hatchway leading onto the dock. As they approached, Connelly could see a few people moving about, some going into the ship carrying boxes and some leaving with other types of gear. If this ship was a regular cargo vessel it seemed that there would be a lot of lights and the sounds of forklifts and other machinery rattling away in support of loading and unloading. This ship almost seemed like a ghost ship preparing for a covert mission.

As they approached the ship, the Korean man hunched a bit and scrutinized the personnel on the pier. He waited for several minutes and then finally saw the person for whom he was apparently looking. He walked very quickly to the beginning of the pier and made his way up the embankment, carrying his baby and helping his wife. Connelly followed and soon they were at the entrance to the pier.

"Ha-neul!" the Korean man said to the sailor.

"Bae!" he replied.

Connelly stood silently and awkwardly as the two men engaged in a quick-paced conversation for a minute or so. The sailor had glanced at Connelly several times during the conversation and finally Bae pointed to Connelly and apparently explained who he was and why he had joined them. Ha-neul paused for a moment then shrugged his shoulders and waved them through onto the pier.

Connelly looked down the pier at the ship and tried to classify it. It was a motor vessel, designed for medium-sized cargo containers. It was in the 15,000 ton class, probably staying local to the Sea of Japan but certainly capable of open-ocean travel. It probably wouldn't need more than a dozen or so crewmen to run it and Connelly started to count the sailors he saw. A couple were in maritime uniforms but another one down the pier was in a military uniform. As they got close, the blood drained from Connelly's face- it was Major Gwon!

Connelly turned his face away and stooped over to hide his six-foot height. He tugged on Bae's sleeve to get his attention. Connelly pointed discreetly at Gwon and then made a hiding gesture that the man understood right away. He quickly reached into his wife's backpack and pulled out a rolled-up hat. Connelly unrolled it and stretched it over his head, tilting the brim towards Gwon's direction. If he continued to stoop over and keep his head down Gwon shouldn't be able to see his face. If he did see him, Connelly was prepared to dive off the pier and take his chances with perils of the ocean; there was no way he would be captured again.

Folding his hands and tucking them inside his tunic, Connelly felt the jade figurine in the fold of fabric and he clutched it tightly. He mimicked Bae's gait and tried, in every way possible, to present himself as a North Korean farmer. He resisted the temptation to look at Gwon to make sure he had not been found out and he took a deep breath when he crossed the threshold of the hatchway and stepped onto the metal floor plating inside the ship.

The corridor was very poorly lit and Connelly did all he could to keep an eye on his host as they walked up several flights of stairs and then back down again, rounding innumerable corners and finally settling down in a storage locker that was about thirty feet on a side.

When it seemed safe, Connelly raised his head just enough to glance around the locker. There were about twenty people altogether, ranging in age from what seemed young teens to people in their thirties. Most were girls and women and only a few young men. Connelly couldn't decide what they all had in common but did notice that the young women were dressed similarly to himself- prison camp clothing.

Several hours went by as the crew unloaded crates and subsequently brought supplies onboard. Finally, the sounds of the mooring gear being detached and stowed, accompanied by the starting of massive diesel engines, signaled their departure and Connelly's heartbeat sped up a bit. With the thud of each gear engagement and whistle of steam relief valves he knew that he was edging away from the hell he had lived in for the past twenty-one months.

CHAPTER 13

Without a view of the sky or horizon, Connelly had no way of telling which direction they were going. After an hour or so he figured they were in blue water, judging by the smooth droning of the diesel engines at cruise power. The ship gently rolled back and forth and pitched only slightly. The sea must be pretty calm in this area and Connelly was actually enjoying the ride, knowing that he was putting distance between himself and the prison camp. One nagging fear, though, was that the distance between himself and Major Gwon was perilously small. He tucked his knees in tightly to his chest and kept his new hat pulled down over his face.

A few hours into the voyage, one of the sailors came into the locker and set a large pot down on the floor. After placing a box full of wooden spoons next to the pot, he left the room. The younger passengers quickly scooted over to the pot and put several scoops of rice into their overturned hats. Although Connelly had eaten more rice in the last twenty-one months than he cared to in a lifetime, he eventually made his was over and took a few scoops into the palm of his hand, wanting to keep his hat on. Despite the lack of variety this meal offered, Connelly was keen to enjoy it since it differed from the camp's rice by being relatively clean and seemingly cooked in somewhat clear water. The taste was pleasantly free of the bitter and unpalatable elements of the camp's rice. Since he hadn't eaten in over twenty-four hours, his stomach craved the nutrition and he had several handfuls before retiring against the bulkhead and nodding off.

CHAPTER 14

Connelly awoke and rubbed his eyes, having no idea how long he had been asleep. The ship was rolling much more now than before and the sound of waves smacking against the hull told him that they were much further out to sea and making good time... to where was another question.

He saw several people leave the locker and head down one of the corridors and he wondered where they were going. A few minutes later they returned and took their places on the floor. When his host got up, he motioned for Connelly to follow him and the two walked down the corridor and turned down another. Shortly, they were in a small room that had several portholes and one of them was open to the ocean. The man walked up to the open porthole and proceeded to relieve himself into the ocean. Connelly understood and followed in turn. While he was urinating into the ocean, Connelly looked carefully at the porthole and figured that in his emaciated state he could probably fit through this one. He just hoped that if a storm came up someone would close it so that the ship didn't flood.

After he had finished, he checked to make sure the figurine of Lauren hadn't fallen out of his tunic and then he followed his host back into the locker. So far it was much better than the camp in terms of food, accommodations, and facilities. The cherry on top was the the promise of a new destination; would it be Hong Kong? Thailand? Maybe Tokyo! In the hours spent on the locker floor he planned out his course of action for every possible destination he could think of. His spirits rose as he found that there weren't any destinations for which he could not come up with a plan. He figured that within two weeks he would be back in the States and in a Navy hospital. Maybe he could convince a nurse to sneak him a steak and... a beer! Yes, a frosty cold beer would be incredible! He quickly fell asleep and dreamed of grilled T-bone steaks, stuffed baked potatoes, an ice-cold thirty-two ounce Heineken, and a big slice of pecan pie. A thin line of drool slipped down his cheek as his saliva glands joined in on the fantasy.

CHAPTER 15

Connelly kept a rough track of how long they had been on the ship by counting sunrises and sunsets when he went to the porthole to pee. It was tough to be sure, given the monotony of his days, but he figured they had been at sea for four full days. At a typical speed of twelve knots, they should have covered about 1,200 miles by now. He could tell by the temperature that they had not gone north so, assuming they weren't going in circles, they should be well south of Honshu, Kyushu, and even Okinawa. Were they making for Australia or turning west for Vietnam or maybe further to India? The only other possibility was... east! If they were heading east, they would be within a thousand miles of Midway Island which is about a thousand miles from Hawaii. No, that couldn't be; how could a North Korean cargo vessel, manned by a half-military, half-civilian crew dock in Hawaii? No, that didn't make sense. Then again, upon contemplation, not much about this trip made sense. Connelly considered his host and the man he knew on the crew that let them aboard, surely knowing that all of them were fugitives of one sort or another. He wondered who all these people were and where they were all going.

CHAPTER 16

On the eighteenth day of the voyage Connelly felt a change. The ship's engines began to slow and there was activity on the deck- he could hear voices barking out orders and gear being slung around. Connelly quickly made his way to the porthole and looked out. It was quite dark outside although he couldn't tell if it late at night or very early in the morning.

The ship made a turn to starboard which unfortunately gave Connelly a view of the ocean they had just crossed. He was desperate to know what was immediately in front of them! No way to find out short of seeking a porthole on the port side of the ship but that might expose his presence to Gwon and ruin his escape. No, he had survived this long and he was determined to make it all the way. He turned to go back to the locker just as several people from the locker arrived to look out the portholes for some clues. He sat back down in the locker and huddled against the bulkhead just as he had for the better part of the last three weeks. The engines settled down into a rough idle and some smaller generators came online. Then a mighty splash told Connelly that the ship had set anchor. A few minutes later, a few of the passengers made their way back but instead of entering the locker they continued on down the corridor. Connelly's host motioned for him to join them and he did so, hiding amongst the dozen or so people. They made their way to the port side of the ship and looked out onto land.

It was tough to tell through the dirty portholes but Connelly could make out that they had set anchor maybe a quarter-mile from a harbor that was quite full and busy, even at this hour. In stark contrast to their point of embarkation, this harbor was glowing in a mighty bath of yellow-tinted sodium lights and the roar of cranes and conveyors could be easily heard even at this distance. Men in hard hats could be seen moving crates around and tending to various tasks. Some small tenders periodically made their way out to the vessels moored nearby but none had come to his ship yet. Connelly could see that the harbor was in a well-populated area complete with large buildings nearby. He strained to see the writing on the side of a building or maybe a large billboard to indicate in which country they had landed, but they were too far away for him to tell. Again, he would have to be patient.

CHAPTER 17

Several hours later he was awoken by the sound of two Korean guards dragging three young women out of the locker. There was some resistance by the girls but for the most part they seem resigned to their fate, whatever exactly it was. As the number of people in the locker dwindled Connelly felt more anxious, realizing that he might be discovered. He slid over a bit into a darker shadow while he considered his options.

An hour later another young woman and a young man were escorted out of the locker and Connelly felt that the time to leave was at hand. He had only come up with one option and it seemed that it was going to have to do. The first part of the plan was to excuse himself to the "restroom".

When he arrived at the porthole there was a man from the locker there just finishing. Connelly took his time sidling up to the adjacent porthole and waited for the man to leave. The moment he was out of sight, Connelly felt the edges of the porthole and stuck his head through to have a look. The drop off to the water's surface was a good thirty feet but there weren't any anchor chains below the porthole and the ship's hull curved inward so it would not interfere with his descent to the water's surface. Connelly pulled his head back through the hole and assessed its diameter, trying to mentally measure it against the width of his shoulders. Two years ago he couldn't have dreamt of squeezing through a porthole but the emaciation he had endured made such feats potentially possible. He leaned in again to try slipping his shoulder through the hole when suddenly a man turned the corner. The man's eyes spread wide as he immediately realized what Connelly was trying to do. Connelly quickly made a grunting sound and grasped his abdomen as though he was having digestive problems- hardly a stretch. He feigned a quick vomit out the porthole and then wiped his forehead as he stepped away from the porthole and sat against the opposite wall, continuing the ruse of digestive sickness. The man shot him a quick glance and then went about his business, intent on ignoring the strange American.

After a minute or so the man had finished and left the corridor. Connelly quickly made his way back to the porthole and slipped his right shoulder through the opening trying carefully to not scrape what little skin he had on the sharp edge of the porthole's frame. With his right arm and shoulder out he maneuvered his head into the hole and scraped his left ear as he slid it through the hole. Given that the muscles in his back had atrophied considerably and his hips had little to no flesh on them, he was almost home. As he began to arrange his left arm so that it could fit through the opening he heard the sound of several men in boots quickly making their way into the corridor. His heart quickened and then almost stopped when two men rushed towards him and grabbed him! One man had his hands on Connelly's ribcage and the other grabbed his feet and pulled. Connelly struggled to free himself but the men were strong and they easily won the fight, yanking his body back through the hole and letting him smack unceremoniously on the steel plate flooring.

Connelly was stunned for a moment and then opened his eyes to see his worst nightmare.

"Mister Johnson!"

Connelly let out an audible groan as he looked the despicable Major Gwon in the face.

"I didn't know you were a guest on our... trip. What a wonderful surprise!" he cackled.

"When I had heard you escaped from the camp I thought you would be dead by now. But you are resourceful. It seems that what I have told you time and time again is true: if you wait with earnest patience the gods of war will pave a golden path for you," he said.

The two men had gotten Connelly to his feet as Gwon closed the distance between them.

"Unfortunately for you, it will not end well. I, however, will have tremendous patience and I will be rewarded when the storms of war power me to victory!" he shouted.

He then belted Connelly in the face, as he had many times before, and Connelly stumbled back several steps before crashing to the steel floor again.

Gwon let out several demonic, bellowing laughs and they resonated in the metal corridor. The guards, somewhat frightened, joined in with some forced laughter.

Connelly, lying on the floor in almost a fetal position, kept a sharp eye on the three men and slowed pulled his legs in and slipped his feet underneath himself, coiled. In a flash he made some decisions and a quick estimate. He resolved to end this one way or the other, right there and then.

When none of the three men were looking directly at him he burst upward with a massive surge of adrenaline and sprung forward towards the porthole. He aimed for the center and extended his right arm in front of him and held his left arm tight against his body, in an almost Superman-like pose. Before the guards could react Connelly had leapt through the porthole.

On the way down, Connelly could already feel his left knee starting to swell from an impact with the porthole frame. His other injuries, a large cut on his left arm and six or eight deep bruises in various places, would need a few minutes to start emitting their painful cries. As he tumbled, he tried to get a sense of how far it was to the water but it was difficult to tell at the still dark hour. After a second or so he figured he must be pretty close and he drew in as deep a breath as his lungs could possibly hold. A moment later the impact with the water's surface stung his back and was quickly followed by the needle-like piercing sensation of the cold water enveloping his body.

He opened his eyes to try to get his bearings but was hopelessly disoriented and unable to see anything. He paused for a moment and then started paddling instinctively in the direction he thought would lead to the surface. The rising pressure in his ears quickly told him it was the wrong direction and he thrashed about in the other direction. His lungs started hurting and he got nervous about drowning. Not after having come this far! Another two tries at swimming towards the surface just frustrated him and he knew he had to clam down and think for a second. He managed to be still and thought long enough to realize that his body, unlike a normal healthy one, was probably negatively buoyant- he would sink naturally. Despair began to set in when he realized that air would rise, so he opened his eyes wide and let some of the precious air in his lungs slip through his lips. Even in the darkness he could see the luminous bubbles accelerate away across his right cheek. Bingo! He reoriented himself and paddled in the direction of the bubbles. He lost sight of the original ones and let a few more slip out to guide him. With every second his lungs burned more fiercely and then suddenly his head breached the water! He used his arms to keep his head above the surface as he took several deep breaths into his vacated lungs.

When Connelly's head popped out of the camouflage of the water, one of the guards pointed his 9mm pistol and began to squeeze the trigger.

"No! You idiot!" Gwon shouted.

"Someone on the dock will see the muzzle flash and hear the report. We don't need the Coast Guard asking questions right now," he said.

With that he slapped the man's hand down and glared out of the porthole at the American that slipped through his fingers... twice.

"I will see Mister Johnson again. I am sure of it," he said.

CHAPTER 18

The swim to shore would have been a pretty easy effort for most people with an athletic background but Connelly struggled to cover every yard of the trip. His lack of fat and terrible muscle condition conspired to drown him when he was within a minute's swim to freedom. He had to spit out a mouthful of saltwater as his breathing and bobbing got uncoordinated. He avoided choking and finally arrived at a metal ladder that extended down from the dock into the slip. He threw his left arm over one of the rungs and grabbed the railing with his right arm as his legs wrapped around the bottom of the ladder. He let out a deep sigh and looked back at the ship.

He couldn't make out any details but he was pretty sure that no one was pursuing him and no additional lights had been turned on him. He was thankful.

It took a good ten minutes for him get up the strength to climb the twenty rungs of the ladder but he did it and, after rolling onto the warm pavement, he lay on his back, spread-eagle for almost fifteen minutes without moving. He began laughing and couldn't stop for another twenty minutes as he went back over the escape from North Korea, his laughs masking the horrendous pain and despair.

Eventually he regained some strength and decided to find out to where he had escaped. He rolled over and looked towards the businesses located at the harbor.

"Holy shit," slipped out of his mouth.

No more than fifty yards away was a sing that read, 'M.J. McCullough and Sons Shipping, Inc.' The address below the name was '649 East Pier, Long Beach, California.'

He was home.

CHAPTER 19

In the hour or so that it took for first light to come over California, Connelly had made his way up the harbor row and found a quiet out-of-the-way place to hide in case anyone from the ship had come ashore looking for him. One advantage of his physical state was that he easily fit inside an empty fifty-five gallon drum and didn't even mind the discomfort of it.

By this time the harbor was buzzing with activity as the main shift arrived to kick the loading and unloading into high gear. Workers wearing hard hats were everywhere, some barking orders and others back-talking supervisors and coworkers alike. The smell of diesel fuel mixed easily with the stench of sewage common in this kind of environment. The clanking sound of forklifts interrupted the foul-mouth swearing of their operators and Connelly delighted in hearing the first genuine American curse words he had heard in years.

He discreetly egressed from the drum and looked himself over. He was covered in soot from the drum, almost hiding the blood stains that ran down his arms which in turn almost hid some of the deep bruises. He couldn't tell how bad he smelled or what his face looked like but he realized there really wasn't a damn thing he could do about it right now. Before he left the storage area he reassured himself that his figurine was still secure in his tunic and then he walked into the light.

He tried to imagine what a normal person would walk like but soon realized that pretty much no one was paying any attention to him. He looked around and saw a beggar on the street corner and figured that the two of them seemed to wear the same uniform. He made his way along the row of shipping company dispatch offices and finally chose one. He stepped through the door to find a beat up room with a table, a dirty couch, and a desk with a man behind it, the dispatcher.

Connelly slowed walked up to the dispatcher and stood in front of the desk.

"Ain't got no work," the dispatcher said without even looking up.

"Uh, no, I'm not looking for work," Connelly said. He looked around for a second, searching for the right thing to say. "I need a phone book, please."

The dispatcher pointed to the table across the room without looking up from his clipboard. Connelly walked over to the table and found the white pages just as a gentle wave of air conditioned air rolled over his back. He closed his eyes and marveled at the wonderful sensation of cool air. After a few seconds he turned his attention back to the white pages and began flipping through the pages, in the "C" section of the residential listings. He found the number he was looking for and scribbled it on a scrap of paper. His handwriting looked atrocious- a combination of lack of writing for years and a menagerie of injuries, but the numbers were legible. He returned to the dispatcher.

"I need to make a phone call, please."

CHAPTER 20

"Hello?" the woman answered.

"Hi. Uh... is Dan there?" Connelly asked.

"Yes, he's here. Who is calling?"

Connelly paused and considered his response.

"This is an old buddy of his... Mike. Mike Randall," he said, recalling the name of an old friend of Dan's.

"OK. Hang on," she said.

A moment later a man's voice came on the line.

"Mike? Is that you, you old son of a bitch?" he asked playfully.

Connelly paused again and took a deep breath.

"Dan, this is AJ. Seriously- it's not a prank. Ask me anything."

On the other end of the line Dan's throat tightened as he contemplated the information. The idea that it was a hoax was very likely but the voice was right on the money.

"Uh, yeah. Who is this?" he asked weakly.

"It's me, Dan. Really. You made out with Anne Black in our parents' bedroom on New Year's Eve when you were thirteen."

Dan's face turned white as the blood drained out of his face. His pulse was racing as he began to believe that the man to whom he was talking on the phone was his brother... who died two years ago.

Unable to speak, Dan weakly handed the phone back to his fiancé who had become quite concerned at Dan's reaction to the phone call.

"Who is this?" she asked sternly.

"I'm Dan's brother, AJ. I'm alive and I'm in Long Beach. I don't know who you are but I assume you know that I was reportedly killed in action flying a mission for the Navy. I survived and just made my way back to the States. Dan's going to have a hard time believing it until he sees me. I need you to come get me."

"Yes, of course I've heard about you. My name is Claudia Foret and Dan and I are engaged," she explained.

Connelly and Claudia talked for a few minutes but Connelly had to cut it short since the dispatcher was beginning to glare at him and motioning for the phone to be returned to its cradle. Connelly told Claudia where he was and asked for her to pick him up.

"OK, I'll... we'll... come pick you up right away," she said.

Connelly waited on the torn-up sofa in the dispatcher's office, soaking in the sights and sounds of the modern, mechanized world he hadn't seen in years. As he relaxed, his body started to awaken to its condition and he started to feel some pain. His feet were swollen and cut up, his lungs hurt, the bruise on his knee was the size of a tennis ball, and his muscles ached all over.

It took about twenty minutes for Claudia to settle Dan down and get him into the car. Dan hadn't said anything coherent since the phone call but the color had started to return to his face. The drive to Long Beach took about an hour and it took another fifteen minutes for her to find a place to park their car in the shipping district.

Finally they found 'McCullough and Sons' and went inside the dispatcher's office. Dan went in first and scanned the room. The dispatcher was behind his desk but aside from a couple of longshoremen and a bum there didn't seem to be anybody else there. When Connelly was about six steps away Dan noticed him approaching. With each subsequent step Dan looked at the man more closely. When he stopped only a couple of feet away, Dan started to see his brother through all the dirt, blood, and bruises on his hollow face. His eyes were bulging a bit, his cheeks sunken, and his lips thin and pale... but it was A.J.

"Oh my god," he whispered as Connelly took the last step forward and gave Dan a hug. Dan could do little more than cough a few words out as his diaphragm was paralyzed with fear that this was an illusion.

"I thought you died," he said.

"Yeah, me too," Connelly replied.

Claudia ushered the two of them out of the dispatcher's office and back towards their car. Dan was in a daze, expressionless and lightheaded. Connelly was more solid but his legs were definitely struggling to get him to the car. Despite the filth covering him, Claudia wrapped an arm around his impossibly thin waist and helped him to the car. She opened the back door of the charcoal gray BMW 740i and placed Connelly in the back seat. Dan blankly got into the front passenger's seat as Claudia got in, started the car, and headed for the freeway. Dan flipped the visor down so that he could see Connelly in the vanity mirror.

Connelly let his battered body sink into the pillow-soft leather upholstery and closed his eyes as he contrasted the smooth-as-glass ride of the 'ultimate driving machine' and the bone-jarring ride in the bed of the little yellow Toyota. For a moment he wondered which was the dream- the North Korean prison camp or this clear, soft, cool place he now was.

"AJ, are you hungry? Do you want a burger?" Claudia asked.

A burger. Wow, what a concept. The thought of a meal that was anything other than cold rice had become foreign to him.

"Yes, I'm hungry."

Claudia pulled off the main road and picked up a burger and fries meal at the In-N-Out drive through. She handed him the bag and almost reflexively asked him to try to not spill on the upholstery but caught herself just in time.

Connelly opened the bag and was mesmerized by the wonderful, captivating scent of french fries. Oh, that wonderful smell! He reached into the bag and yanked out a handful of fries and shoved them in his mouth. The oil burned his tongue, cheeks, and palette but he didn't care- without a flinch he chewed the mouthful of potatoes and swallowed. Delicious! He devoured the rest of the fries in a minute flat and moved on to the burger. Meat! Besides one Christmas when Shin gave him a pencil-sized piece of smoked yak he hadn't had meat since the night before he flew his mission. The burger was dripping with mustard and the tomato had nearly slid out of the sandwich altogether. The rings of onion were sloppily strewn on top of the patty and the lettuce rubbed the side of his mouth as he jammed it in for a bite. He rolled his head back and moaned as he savored the taste of this amazing food treat. In a minute he finished off the burger and slurped down the large-sized Coke. Bliss.

Ten minutes later, as Claudia was transitioning from one interstate to another, Connelly spoke up urgently.

"Claudia, pull over."

"Why?"

"Just pull over, now," Connelly said as he started to buckle forward.

Claudia had barely stopped the car when Connelly stumbled out of the back seat and dropped onto his hands and knees. As quickly as they had gone down, the burger and fries came back up and were deposited scattershot onto the shoulder of the 710.

After a minute or so, with Claudia holding his shoulders, Connelly stopped vomiting and lay down on the pavement.

"Are you OK?" she asked.

Connelly had covered his eyes with his hands to block out the sun.

"Yeah, I'm OK. I think I ate too fast. And too much."

"It may take some time for your system to adjust," she offered.

She managed to wipe the vomit off of his face and got him back in the car. The rest of the trip was uneventful but Connelly's hunger was returning by the time the BMW came to rest in the parking deck of Dan and Claudia's condo complex. The three of them went into the condo and Connelly looked around at all the nice things they had- a TV, a beautiful suede sofa, and some tasteful pieces of artwork on the walls. He also noticed a gorgeous black panther carved out of obsidian resting on a mahogany stand.

"I'll see if I've got something plain in the pantry. Maybe some rice," Claudia offered as she helped Connelly sit on a chair.

"No. No, please. No rice," Connelly said with startling force. "Anything else."

Dan was sitting in a chair a few feet away from Connelly and stared at him in disbelief.

"AJ, I... I can't believe you're alive. The Navy told us that you were killed. I'm so sorry!"

"It's OK, Dan. Really, it's OK," he assured his weeping brother.

"AJ, we had your funeral!" he squealed with his jar clenched tight.

Connelly got up and went over to his little brother. He put his hand on Dan's shoulder and told him that it was all right.

"I understand. I know this is really hard. Just take it easy," he said.

He stayed there for a few minutes as tears ran down Dan's face. A few minutes later Claudia came back into the room with a plate and a glass in her hands.

"Some white toast with a little butter. And a glass of tap water," she said as she offered the modest meal to him. Connelly sat back down and started into the toast much more cautiously this time as Claudia tended to Dan.

CHAPTER 21

Several hours later, Dan had managed to lie down on the sofa in such a way that he could keep an eye on his miraculously present brother. Connelly had given Dan and Claudia the short version of what happened to him, describing the ejection from the U-2 and the rhythmic trips to the mountain camp. He avoided descriptions of the beatings that had obviously taken place and the lack of sanitation that had ravaged him. It seemed to help Dan a lot to hear the story as it began to fill in a big gap in the last two years for him as well. Connelly started to tire and told them he would tell them more about it later.

"Well, do you want to take a bath?" Claudia offered.

"Wow, a bath," he muttered. "Yeah, that would be great."

His legs were weak and his bruised knee had essentially rendered his leg stiff. Claudia helped him into the bathroom and turned on the water to fill the tub. She selected a very mild-scented bath gel to put in the water. She placed a couple of towels next to the tub and started to leave. She looked back as she was about to pass through the doorway and saw Connelly struggling to get his arm through the hole in the tunic. She took a deep breath and looked him over. He looked like a car wreck victim. She started to get Dan but quickly realized he had fallen fast asleep, completely exhausted from the emotional surge of the day. She bit her lip and went back into the bathroom.

Without saying a word, she gently grabbed Connelly's right arm and helped him slip it through the hole in the tunic. After the left arm was though she slipped the dirty, torn piece of fabric up over his head to expose an emaciated, beaten, naked man. The scars across his chest made her cringe and the sharp protrusions in his ribcage were immediately identified by her as broken ribs that hadn't set properly. Her heart skipped a beat at the image of abuse and her eyes started to well up. She dropped the tunic on the floor.

"Oh, wait!" Connelly said as he awkwardly dropped to his knees and grabbed the garment. He frantically pulled the makeshift belt away and unfolded the material, grasping the jade figurine tightly in his pencil-thin fingers.

"Thank God!" he said as he gently placed the sculpture on a small table in the bathroom.

Claudia hardly noticed the figurine and instead stared at the long lines of scar tissue crisscrossing his back, blending in with the fresh bruises and twisted spine. He was a wreck. After placing the figurine on the table, Connelly looked back at Claudia and she snapped out of her daze.

She placed her hands one the sides of his ribcage to help him up but was afraid to squeeze too hard for fear of crushing the man's torso altogether. Together they managed to get him to his feet and she stabilized him as he stepped into the tub.

Warm water. Connelly paused and closed his eyes again as the marvelous sensation was bestowed upon him. He got the other foot in the tub and stood there, just absorbing the moment. After a minute or so Claudia helped him sit down in the tub and placed a cushion behind his head as he reclined in the tub.

The soap attacked the muck on his feet furiously but was clearly outmatched. Claudia has taken a small towel and wetted it with soapy water. She very gently rubbed his arms and wrung out the towel frequently. Within ten minutes the bath water was overcome with dirt, blood, dead skin, and only God knows what else. Claudia had to reach delicately between Connelly's legs to open the drain and then replace the water in the tub. She continued wiping him down with the soapy towels, changing the water twice more before changing it one last time to let him enjoy the warmth and sensation of the bath.

He was lying back with his head on the cushion and breathing deeply- probably asleep. She thought to leave him alone for some peace and quiet but stayed when she realized that he might slip and drown. She stayed there for forty more minutes, sitting on the tile floor next to the broken man who would soon be her brother-in-law. Despite his wretched condition and having known him for only a few hours, she liked him and felt a respect for him already.

CHAPTER 22

After fourteen hours of blissful sleep, Connelly woke at noon the next day to the sound of coffee being ground. The wonderful aromatic impact of ground coffee stirred his senses and reminded him of his childhood in which the sound of coffee being ground was ubiquitous. When he opened his eyes he could see Dan peering into the guest bedroom where Claudia had deposited Connelly.

"Hey, how do you feel?" Dan asked.

"Different," Connelly replied.

After Dan helped him get up and get dressed, he tried his second meal stateside, this time toast with some peanut butter on it and a glass of ice water with a few drops of lemon juice in it. Claudia had learned the previous day's lesson. Three slices with peanut butter and four glasses of water later Connelly felt satisfied... and gastricly stable. Connelly asked Dan and Claudia how they met and what the plans were for the wedding. They answered the questions with their excitement poking through only occasionally from the weight of Connelly's reappearance. Claudia began telling Connelly about the muscum in Seattle where the wedding was going to take place when she was interrupted by the door bell. Dan explained a little more about how he met Claudia while she answered the door, returning with a man in a casual dress coat and neatly trimmed hair.

"AJ, I've asked a friend of mine to drop by. This is Doctor Martin," she said.

"AJ, I'm Larry Martin. Claudia asked me to come by and give you a look-over. She said you've had... a rough time."

Connelly got up out of the chair and shook the doctor's hand.

"Yes, Doctor, you could say that," he replied.

"Let's use the bedroom as a makeshift exam room."

After the two of them left the living room Dan turned to Claudia with a concerned look.

"What do you think he'll find?" he asked worriedly.

"I have no idea- he looks OK, I mean, all things considered. I don't know," was the best she could offer.

"Have you gotten in touch with Doctor Alden?" she asked.

"Yeah, I talked to him- he's doing a couple of cavities and a bridge this morning but he said we could come by later this afternoon. He'll call when he's available," Dan said.

About forty-five minutes later Doctor Martin returned to the living room with Connelly.

"Given what he's been through, I'd say AJ is in remarkably good health. That is, of course, given that he's been through hell," he said with a weak smile as Connelly sat down.

The doctor described to three of them the injuries he observed and correlated most of them with what Connelly described being done to him. He prescribed a whole pad full of prescriptions for antibiotics, vitamin supplements, and other various treatments. He also wrote out some notes on what Connelly could do to help heal some of his injuries and begin to rebuild his physique and stamina.

"It's going to take a while to recover but I don't see any permanent injuries that are going to inhibit normal function. Please do the things that I've recommended and let me see you again in two weeks."

"Sounds fair. Thank you, Doctor," Connelly said as he again shook the man's hand.

Doctor Martin got up and Claudia escorted him to the door while Connelly discussed what the doctor said with Dan.

"Jesus, Claudia, you said he got lost on a camping trip when we talked on the phone!"

"Well, I didn't think you'd come if I told you he was a POW for two years. Thanks for coming," she said.

Doctor Martin took a deep breath.

"Normally, I would call the police if a patient came into the ER with these kinds of wounds. He said he was shot down in Asia... I don't know what to do with that scenario."

"Just don't do anything right now, OK? He's got enough problems without the media and the police hounding him. I really appreciate your looking at him, but please don't say anything for a couple of weeks. We're going to get him straightened out and when he's better we'll address the legalities."

The doctor took another deep breath and glanced at Connelly as he exhaled.

"All right, I'll keep it quiet... for a while. Besides, I really appreciate the deal you found for me on my house, so I owe you this one."

Claudia smiled and gave him a brief hug then let him out. She had known Larry for years and was glad to have made a good friend with a doctor. Fortunately, Dan had gotten to know a dentist through his golf club and took Connelly to see him later that afternoon. Not surprisingly, there were serious signs of dental neglect but nothing that couldn't be solved with a half-dozen visits. Everyone agreed that he would wait until his health had recovered and then proceed with the more serious treatments. In the meantime a return to brushing twice a day and flossing would do wonders for him.

Two days later Connelly had progressed to ham sandwiches and one cup of coffee a day. Doctor Martin's advice included some stretches and basic strength exercises which he started to do. It was a week before Dan returned to work at his law office and Claudia started working half-days shortly thereafter. A month later Connelly was walking quite well and started helping with tasks around the house and making trips to the convenience store which was two blocks away. The walking felt good and he was acclimating to the 'new' life fairly quickly.

"So, AJ, how are you feeling today?" Claudia asked as she came through the door with a grocery bag in one arm.

"Good... and a little restless. I think it may be time to take the next step," he said.

Claudia put down the bag and sat next to Connelly on the couch.

"What do you mean?" she asked.

"Well, I've got to get back into the swing of things... start to rebuild my life," he said.

Claudia didn't know what to say right away and sat silent for a few moments.

"You're welcome to stay here as long as you need or want, you know that, right?" she said.

"Yes, I do. Thank you for your kindness, but I've got to get going and let you two get on with your life," he said.

"AJ, you're part of our life."

"Oh, I know. Don't worry- I'm not disappearing again!" he said.

They talked for a half hour until Dan came home and then the three of them discussed what Connelly was thinking and what he would do next.

In the morning, Dan pulled the BMW up next to the curb and put the gearshift in park.

"You sure you don't want me to come in? I know some lawyers we could bring along, you know, to throw some weight around," Dan said.

"I appreciate it, Dan, but the Navy doesn't really care about civilian lawyers. This is going to take some military-bullshit talking and throwing around some jargon and dropping a couple of names that, hopefully, still mean something," he said.

"I understand. I'll be right out here if you need anything."

"Thanks," Connelly said as he got out of the car wearing a white button-down shirt and black slacks that Dan had bought him the day before. With a haircut and his first good shave he looked almost like a Naval officer as he strode into the Point Mugu Naval Air Station's checkpoint.

"Can I help you, Sir?" asked the seaman behind the desk.

"Yes, I'm Commander Andrew Connelly. I need to see the officer on duty right away," he barked out in a tone of voice designed to grab the young enlisted man's attention.

"Yes Sir, Commander, right away," he said as he picked up the phone.

"Lieutenant Grayson, please come to the front," he said.

A minute later the young officer appeared in the front office and squared up to Connelly.

"Can I help you?"

"Yes, Lieutenant, I'm Commander Andrew Connelly and I need you to patch me through to the CINCPAC office immediately," he ordered.

"May I see your identification, Sir?"

"No, I don't have my ID on me," he replied evenly.

"I'm sorry Sir, without ID I cannot contact CINCPAC for you."

"Lieutenant, my ID was stowed before my last assignment and I'm trying to retrieve it. That's the problem."

"Well, if you can produce some sort of ID, civilian maybe, birth certificate, Starbuck's card, anything with your name on it, I'll be happy to help you. Until then, I suggest you leave," he said.

Connelly took a deep breath.

"Lieutenant, what's the smallest infraction for which you would book someone?"

"I suppose that would be disorderly conduct or maybe vandalism; why do you ask?"

Connelly turned without responding and strode across the room. He picked up a steel frame chair and threw it through the window leading into the lieutenant's office. In about thirty seconds two beefy sailors were on Connelly, cuffing his hands behind his back. They had an easy time getting him into a back room since he was offering no resistance. Sitting in the small room with an armed Shore Patrolman staring at him produced a feeling in his gut that reminded him of a few months ago. Suddenly this didn't seem like such a great idea. He kept reminding himself that things would be OK soon.

About thirty minutes later he was put in the back of an SUV and driven to the main security facility on the base. As Connelly stretched his legs in the back of the Ford he noticed that the air conditioning was running and the windows were tinted, reducing the glare of the sun to a comfortable level. What luxury compared to the little yellow pickup.

After a couple of hours waiting in the processing room at the security facility he was finally admitted into an office with a petty officer nearing retirement.

"What did you do, son? Bar fight?" he asked almost fatherly.

"No, chief. I'm Commander Connelly. I've lost my ID and I need you to fingerprint me and run it through the Naval Intelligence computer. Try the name I'm telling you and this will go real fast," he said.

The petty officer had never heard that one but felt no need to delay the course of action suggested to him. About fifteen minutes later the petty officer had confirmed Connelly's identity but was perplexed by his status being listed as 'Killed In Action'.

"Well, when they transfer you from Atlantic Command to Pacific Command and then you get reassigned through three different other commands it's inevitable that some clerk is going to find it easier to press the 'KIA' button than process your paperwork. I'm sure you've been there," he said.

The chief smiled a knowing smile and was willing to give Connelly the benefit of the doubt. He issued Connelly a temporary ID card but told him that he would still be listed KIA in the database until he straightened it out. Connelly thanked him and offered to pay for the broken window as a gesture of good will.

"Don't worry about it. That LT is a real son-of-a-bitch and it serves him right. He'll have to deal with the requisition officer and he doesn't like him either. Don't worry about it. You need a ride back to the checkpoint?"

"Yeah, please."

The petty officer dropped him off right next to Dan's car and wished him well, clearly a veteran of the Navy's red tape and a sympathetic soul.

A couple of hours later, in a large office in Washington DC, there was a knock on the austere mahogany door.

"Come."

A young lady in a gray suit with short black heels and hair pulled back tightly strode into the office of Mack Jurgensen and handed him a print out and then quickly left.

Jurgensen finished signing the papers he was working on and then looked at the note. When his eyes read that a man claiming to be AJ Connelly had roughed up a checkpoint at a Navy base in California that morning his pulse quickened and he got a knot in his stomach.

CHAPTER 23

"Gwon, my son, the gods of war and prosperity came to me last night and have shown me your path to redemption," General Seong said to Major Gwon.

Gwon bowed his head in shame over having lost the American prisoner. He had been called to General Seong's palace high in the mountains near Namp'o and had feared that this would be his dismissal. The turn of fortune, in the form of a path to redemption, stirred a fire of hope in his belly.

"Yes, General, I will do anything."

"I know, Gwon," the General said as he motioned for them to walk together along a stone path leading from the palace's main foyer out into the brilliant afternoon. The view from the palace was stunning, overlooking a rugged but alluring forest.

"Gwon, our country is in need," the general said.

"It is a great country! Once its shackles have been removed its glory will enlighten the world!" Gwon protested.

"Yes, you are right," the General calmly agreed. "And it will be your goal to break those shackles, removing the constraints on our vision and our people, allowing us to take our proper place at the head of the world's resources."

Gwon, nodding furiously, responded quickly.

"Yes, General, I will do it. I will forge the path that the gods of war and prosperity have dictated for me."

"The path is a long path, for the goal is mighty. To remove the immoral oppression put upon us will take great strength, since it will take a mighty blow to sever the bindings," the general explained.

"I am equal to any task required to free our people!" Gwon enthused.

"That is good, for you will be required to accomplish tasks of great difficulty and patience, requiring guile and foresight."

General Seong told Major Gwon to return three days hence, at which time he would reveal the details of the plan that the gods of war and prosperity had bestowed upon him and his charge.

CHAPTER 24

"You really don't have to go," Dan told his brother.

"I appreciate it, really, but it's time to get on with reestablishing my life and starting something new," Connelly said.

"Yeah, but we're family, you could live here in Long Beach."

"We'll always be family and we'll visit each other frequently, but I've got to let you get on with your relationship with Claudia and your career. I'm going to head back to Stovall, I think, and try to start over."

"You know, they say you can never go home," Dan said.

Connelly nodded at the aphorism.

"Well, at least it's familiar and it's a starting place. I'm not going to try to recapture my childhood life... I'm going to build a new life."

Dan and AJ hugged and AJ thanked Claudia for everything she had done. They made their pledges to stay in touch and even planned a get together in a few months. Connelly promised that he'd repay the money they loaned him as soon as he could but they told him to not worry about it. In addition to several thousand dollars in cash and a credit card they had secured for him, they bought him a train ticket to Washington D.C. and took him to the AmTrak station.

"A nice train ride across the country will be fun," Claudia remarked.

"Yes, it will be scenic and, frankly, my last plane ride had a rough landing so I'm looking forward to staying on the ground," Connelly replied.

There were weak chuckles at Connelly's reference to ejecting over North Korea but it didn't do much to ease Dan's pain at seeing his brother leave again.

"Don't worry, Dan, I'll be OK and I won't disappear again. I'll see you soon," he reassured him.

After a final round of hugs, Connelly hopped aboard the train and settled into his cabin. Dan and Claudia had bought him the finest passage on the train and Connelly looked forward to the trip even though another fight would begin when he reached Washington D.C.

CHAPTER 25

Connelly checked into the Fairmont hotel near Washington Circle in the heart of D.C. The hustle and bustle of the political center of the country had an intensity that shocked Connelly a bit at first. For all its horror, the prison camp had been very quiet and the tension he felt there was of the long-grind type rather than the shooting-star-burn-out roar of D.C. He spent an hour or so in the hotel room, breathing deeply and settling down after the frenetic cab ride. He took a shower and had a nice meal in the hotel's restaurant downstairs. Even after spending two months in Long Beach at his brother's very nice condominium, the luxury of the Fairmont impressed him. The restaurant had a lounge replete with felt-covered wingback chairs and a library. The floors were spotless and the manners impeccable. A long cry from being pistol-whipped by Gwon. He retired to his room early and slept deeply.

He arose early and spent an extra long time getting ready in the morning. While battledress in Korea was dirty camos and a cap, battledress in Washington was spit-polished shoes and an impeccable shave. He had bought a stunning $1,600 suit in Long Beach, a red silk Armani tie, and a pair of black Allen Edmonds to complete the look. When he looked in the mirror the only reflection of his former POW-self that he recognized was the hollow cheeks and scar tissue. He had healed a great deal, thanks largely to an doctor-tailored diet and a dozen visits to the finest medical professionals in California. He felt good but started to get butterflies in his stomach when he asked the cab driver to drop him off at the front door of the NSA.

Once inside, he passed through a metal detector and made his way to the receptionist sitting behind a semicircular marble desk.

"Yes Sir, may I help you?" she asked perfunctorily.

"I'm here to see Mack Jurgensen," Connelly said.

"Do you have an appointment?" she asked.

"No."

"I'm sorry, Mister Jurgensen doesn't—"

Connelly interrupted the woman mid-sentence, leaning onto the desk and towering over her with his six-foot tall frame. "Call him now and tell him that AJ Connelly is here to see him. I'm sure he'll send me up."

She stared back at him, studying his scowl, and decided that he was serious and warranted at least a call upstairs. She punched Jurgensen's number into her phone without looking at the dialing pad.

"Sir, there is a *gentleman* here to see you without an appointment," she said and was interrupted by Jurgensen on the other side. "Yes Sir, I told him that but he told me to tell you that his name is 'AJ Connelly'."

Several seconds of silence were followed by a quick answer from Jurgensen.

"The Associate Director will see you, Mister Connelly. Sign in here and I'll give you a badge," she said.

After the necessary sign-in procedures were taken care of Connelly got into the elevator and rode up to the ninth floor.

When Connelly burst through his office doors, Jurgensen did not even look up and dismissed the receptionist who was franticly protesting Connelly's unapproved entrance and pleading with her boss that she insisted he not enter. She closed the doors behind her after she left the room.

"So, thank God you made it out, AJ!" Jurgensen said as he stood with a broad smile on his face.

Connelly had no such friendly visage and only glowered at Jurgensen for a few seconds before he spoke.

"You, motherfucker, owe me," he said, wiping the smile off Jurgensen's face.

"Watch your mouth, mister. And what the hell do you mean?"

"You left me hanging out to dry. You knew I was a POW and you didn't do a damn thing to help me. I spent almost two years in a cell the size of a doghouse, eating dirt and drinking piss to stay alive, and you didn't do shit."

"Hey, not my problem, err, I mean, my jurisdiction. I tried to get you out, but, it was General Harrison who, I mean, we *wanted* to but, you know..." his voice trailed off as Connelly closed the distance between them, his eyes locked on Jurgensen like a cheetah stalking his prey on the Serengeti.

"I lost two years of my life that I'll never get back but, at least, you're going to give me a jump-start on getting my life back together," Connelly said, his face only inches away from a visibly shaken Jurgensen.

"And how do you want me to do that? I mean, I don't have to do shit for you and what the hell are you going to do about it, anyway? Beat me up? I'll have security here so fast you'll be—"

Connelly cut him off before he could finish his undoubtedly lame threat. "You're going to reinstate my identity then give me a big, fat check that covers all my back pay, plus combat duty, plus POW supplement, plus an early retirement bonus. I also want to retire as a captain, with a twenty-five year service pension beginning to pay out immediately. *That's* what you're going to do."

"That's ridiculous. I don't have to do that and I won't. Again, I ask, 'what are you going to do about it?'" was Jurgensen's reply.

"I'll find a young, eager reporter for the Washington Post and I'll tell him everything, emphasizing the part about how you knew I was there and you covered it up, leaving a U.S. serviceman hostage and not doing a damn thing because it might tarnish your record and slow your next promotion. Can't wait to see how the public would crucify you and the Agency, not to mention what the Director will do to you for fucking this up so badly. It seems like a few well-deserved dollars to make me go away is quite the bargain for you, shithead."

"You wouldn't tell the press. You'd be court-martialed and spend the rest of your pathetic days rotting is a 'doghouse-sized' cage at Leavenworth."

"Court-martial who? AJ Connelly? He's dead, remember? Good luck trying to pull that one off- the lawyers will have a field day with you trying to prosecute a man that *you* listed as dead."

Jurgensen circled his desk twice and then stared out the one-way window of his office. Without turning back to AJ he gave his answer.

"Leave the name of the bank and your account number with my secretary. The money will be there day after tomorrow. Now get out of here."

CHAPTER 26

As Connelly got off the bus in Raleigh, North Carolina he spotted a taxicab and immediately hailed it. He had the cabbie drop him off at an upscale used car lot and he spent about twenty minutes perusing the options. He zeroed in on an eight year old Range Rover that had some small scratches and a few broken pieces of trim but otherwise looked in solid shape. During the test drive he found the acceleration quite good and the interior appointments nice but not sickly clean. The four-wheel-drive option appealed to him as did the cargo volume and he bought the car right away.

His first stop was at a gas station to fill up the tank and get a road map. Even though he had grown up nearby it had been long enough that he didn't quite remember all the turns. It took about an hour and a half to reach the town where he grew up, Stovall, North Carolina. As he approached from the south on highway 15 he felt his shoulders relax as the landscape, scents, and sounds of his childhood reappeared. On the outskirts of town he passed the old fire station, crossed the small bridge that he and his brother used to jump from on hot summer days when the stream below was a welcomed source of cool entertainment. The middle of town looked rather familiar, the shops and buildings still there with the expected change of name here and there.

As he slowly cruised through the town of 600 residents he noticed many people taking note of his presence. There wasn't much tourism in Stovall and it really wasn't on the way to anywhere so a new face was something significant. He intentionally avoided his parents' old house fearing that something had happened to it or that the urge to 'go home again' might be overwhelming. He parked the Rover near the small courthouse and walked through the quad slowly, breathing in the wonderful, real pine-scented air and listening as the breeze rustled through the needle-covered limbs. With the sun shining down on his face he sat on a bench, closed his eyes and smiled for the better part of a half-hour. Thoughts of his childhood, farther gone than the actual years that had elapsed, raced back through his mind as he replayed his first dating experience and various other significant acts of his youth.

Finally, he collected himself and walked towards the courthouse, entering the unguarded door that led to a receptionist's desk.

"Yes Sir, may I help you?" asked the woman.

"I'm looking for Mayor Tollison. Is he in?" Connelly asked.

"Oh sure, Bob's back from lunch and probably sitting in his office with his feet propped up on his desk. I'll check," she said.

"There's a man here to see you..." she said into the intercom.

"Send him back," came the cheery response.

Connelly walked down a well-worn wooden floored hallway directly into the mayor's office which was relatively small but nicely finished in local furniture. When Connelly saw the same man still running Stovall after all these years he couldn't help but smile. Mayor Tollison slid his feet off of his desk and popped up to meet Connelly with a big smile and outstretched hand.

"I'm Mayor Tollison. Pleased to meet you," he said.

Connelly grinned and paused for a second before responding.

"We've met, Mayor. You may remember me from the time that Tommy and I tore that gutter off the back of your house trying to break our fall when we slipped off the roof."

Tollison took a few seconds to dig up the memory of that particular escapade of his son's but the moment it did, a large grin stretched from ear to ear.

"Holy shit, you're Andy! I recognize you now! How are you?" he asked energetically.

"Just great. It's great to back in Stovall," he said genuinely.

"Wow, how long has it been?" the mayor asked.

"About sixteen years, I'd say," Connelly replied.

The two of them spent about a half-hour discussing the basics about the disposition of various family members and what Connelly had been doing since he graduated high school. Connelly gave polite but somewhat guarded answers and completely skipped the North Korean detour and simply explained that he had been in the Navy until just a few months ago.

"So what brings you to Stovall?" the mayor asked.

"Well, I'm thinking about starting over... you know, getting back to where I started. I enjoyed growing up here and thought it would be nice to come back 'home' and get something going."

"There's not a lot going on in Stovall, but it's still a really nice place and we'd be happy to have you back," the mayor replied.

"We've got a few new houses down on Billiard Street and 'Old Man Jenkins' has been thinking about selling his place for a while. I could talk to him, if you want to," the mayor offered.

Connelly nodded a few times and looked blankly around the Mayor's office.

"What about Station 65? I saw it on the way in," Connelly stated quizzically.

"The old fire station? It's been abandoned for a couple of years, ever since the county took over fire service. We've thought about tearing it down, but those bastards from Granville County want fifty-thousand just to tear it down and haul the debris away! We don't have that kind of money in our budget so we decided to just leave it be. It's an unpleasant sight but it's out of the way," he explained, referring to the station's location being about a half-mile outside of town.

Connelly looked the mayor straight-on and made him an offer.

"How about this- we help each other out. You give me the deed to the station and have it re-zoned for residential use. In return I'll promise to completely renovate the place, inside and out, so it'll look real nice for people passing by- it'll restore a bit of Stovall's heritage and take care of your eyesore at a savings of fifty grand. What do you say?" Connelly asked.

The mayor leaned back in his seat and gazed hard at Connelly, assessing the likelihood that he would do as he said he would. Mayor Tollison had known Connelly's parents for years and held them in high esteem. He also appreciated that Connelly had been in the Navy and felt that made him more reliable than the average 'Joe'. He finally concluded that he really had nothing to lose in this arrangement.

"OK, Mister Connelly, that sounds like a fair trade. I can't give you the station, however, since it's public property," he said.

Connelly was a little concerned about what sort of price tag was going to be put on the old station.

"How about one dollar?" the mayor offered with a big grin.

Connelly stuck his hand out, shaking the Mayor's.

"That's a deal!" Connelly said.

The mayor agreed to have the necessary papers drawn up and ready in a couple of days. He took Connelly into one of the store rooms and dug through an old cardboard box full of junk and finally came up with the keys to the front door of the station.

"I'll have Mickey turn on the power and water service and tell them to get the garbage truck to come up there on Thursdays. Can't say I know what kind of condition it's like on the inside- you might be in for a long haul," the mayor cautioned.

"A long haul is just what I'm looking for," Connelly replied.

Having concluded the negotiations with much less trouble than he had anticipated, Connelly happily drove up Cameron Road and pulled onto the gravel road that ran thirty yards into the woods where the station rested.

Station 65 was built in the 1950s from red clay bricks. It was about seventy feet wide and just as deep with two full stories and an accessible roof that featured an observation dome used for spotting fires in the distance when the station was employed as a firefighting base. The front of the building was dominated by the thirty-foot wide roll-up door that allowed entry and exit for the fire engine. It was dirty but, remarkably, all of the window panes were intact. A pedestrian entrance was next to the roll-up door and a few windows adorned the front wall. On the second floor were a pair of windows that no doubt looked into a lounge area and perhaps a sleeping quarter. Connelly was excited about the prospects of designing the interior to suit his needs.

Inside, he found the expected indications of abandonment- a moldy smell, cobwebs, and dingy walls. The first floor had a large bay for the truck and numerous storage cabinets for gear that would have been used on the truck. Some pieces of maintenance equipment remained behind as well as some tools that still looked usable. The rest of the ground floor consisted of a kitchen and a living area with a couch that would need to be thrown away immediately. The linoleum floor was beat-up and dirty and would need to be replaced. Connelly was able to see through the dirt and dings and had already imagined a fairly detailed idea of what it would look like after he had renovated the place. Structurally it looked solid and he did not hesitate to ascend the spiral staircase leading up the second floor. As he climbed the stairs he eyed the 'fire pole' with a boyish excitement, anticipating the ride back down to the ground floor.

The upstairs had two rooms that would serve well as bedrooms and two other rooms that would function quite well as an entertainment room and a study. Additionally there were several rooms that allowed for extensive storage and special use. It was plain but that would allow him to be extremely creative. He walked around the expansive upper floor and found the ladder leading up the observation dome.

The dome was very dusty and had some water damage as a result of a tree limb smashing through two of the window panes. He grabbed the limb, snapped it into smaller pieces and tossed them through the missing windows onto the roof. The dome was circular and had cabinets on the floor up to knee-height all the way around. There was an access door to the roof that Connelly was able to force open. The roof was designed for people to walk around but there was no railing to hold onto. Connelly surveyed North Carolina for miles and miles and inhaled deeply with the knowledge that he had made a great choice.

CHAPTER 27

Major Gwon returned to General Seong's palace at the duly appointed time to discuss the plan for their return to power and glory. Deep in the bowels of the general's fortress was a well-protected strategy room that reeked of cigar smoke and spilt liquor. Clearly many nights of 'strategizing' had given way to smoking, drinking, and passing out. The room was multifunctional.

On the desk in front of the two men were several maps, a folder, and some notepads, dimly lit in the room's pale lighting.

"Here, about fifty kilometer southwest of Baikonaur," the General said as he pointed at a map of Kazakhstan, "is the development site. Six years ago President Hussein contracted for the development of the RG weapon. They were about one year from delivery when the president was unjustly attacked and removed from power. As such, he was unable to make the final payments for the completion and delivery of the weapon."

"What happened to it?" Gwon asked excitedly.

"It is still in the development facility. The Kazaks have quietly offered it for sale on the black market. When we first heard of its availability, we contracted our Iranian friends to secure it for us. They have managed to convince the Kazaks to reserve the weapon for us by paying them the final payment. In turn, we have to pay our Iranian friends for their loan, help, and eventually delivering the weapon to us."

"This is an excellent plan. Where am I to pick up the weapon?" Gwon asked. The general leaned back in his chair, away from the maps.

"Unfortunately, the treachery of the world's infidels have made it difficult for us. You will need to liberate the money that is rightly ours for use in this purchase. The immoral theft of money from the righteous has filled the pockets of our enemies through their despicable treachery, disguised as trade. The first part of your mission, as shown me by the gods of war and prosperity, will be to collect these moneys. You will do this when the infidels are on our land, the land of the oceans! They have no right to trespass on our waters and you will take that opportunity to recover what is ours. You will then use it to purchase the RG weapon and ultimately use it on our enemy, the holder of the key to our shackles. The weapon will release us from this bondage and allow us to take our proper place."

Gwon's eyes glowed with desire and his blood boiled as he filled with passion for the tasks ahead of him. His fiery eyes trained on his ultimate target and, if they could, would have bored a hole straight through the city encircled on the map - Washington, D.C.

CHAPTER 28

For the first month that Connelly had been back in Stovall he sank his efforts into renovating the old firehouse, Station 65. He liked the idea of living in a place that had a name of its own and decided to refer to his new home as 'Station 65'. After a few days in the local Motel 6, he was able to move into Station 65 because the power and water had been turned on. He spent most of the initial effort clearing out old debris and cleaning up. The big box stores like Home Depot and Lowe's had not made it to Stovall yet so he became friends with the owner of the local hardware store, Gray's, and a few other similar shops in the area. He bought a slightly used refrigerator from the owner of the diner/coffee shop, Benson's, and got a significant discount for promising that he'd frequent the diner. Greg Benson's daughter, Suzy, worked every day in the diner and got to liking Connelly because of his quiet demeanor and reserved self-confidence.

The first room of Station 65 that Connelly renovated was the garage. Most people would have attacked the bedroom first but Connelly's needs for luxurious accommodations had not progressed very far from his days in the POW camp. He slept on a modest mattress, set on the floor and covered with a nice but not extravagant wool blanket. The garage, however, was necessary since he occasionally worked on his Range Rover and had a feeling that he might set up a small workshop there utilizing the tools left by the fire department as a starting point.

After a month Connelly had the garage settled and began to work on other areas of the station. He finally got a bedframe and box springs to put his mattress on and had purchased a small chest of drawers to hold his meager collection of clothes.

He painted the walls a sea green color to be compatible with the wilderness surroundings but not too dark so as to be depressing. A little work in the kitchen produced a functional space that included an oven/stove, toaster oven, and a microwave oven. The fridge slowly began to fill in with items stretching beyond a six-pack of beer and condiments. His diet was slowly returning to its pre-Korea state although he had definitely focused more on healthy foods, purchasing more vegetables and experimenting a little bit with various casseroles and ethnic asian noodle-based dishes. The burgeoning pride of Station 65, however, was two floors up.

On a crisp fall morning, Connelly ventured into the observation dome with replacement windows and lots of cleaning supplies. He started at 6:00 am, installing the new windows and stripping the floors. He worked until midnight, preparing every surface in the room for a complete overhaul. He worked the 6:00 am -midnight schedule for seventeen straight days until the observation dome was immaculately restored. The windows glistened in the sunlight, transparent except for the reflections they cast. The floors, he found out, were mahogany and he researched the proper method for restoring them and spared no expense in using the highest quality materials available to restore and protect them. The cabinets were made from oak and he lavished them with the same care and dedication as he did the floor in returning them to pristine condition. On the last day of renovating the dome he went to an antique furniture store an hour away from Stovall and purchased an extraordinary oak display table that had a twenty-eight inch round top and a three-legged pedestal. It was a gorgeous piece that fit into the decor of the room perfectly. He positioned it against the wall and directly in front of the staircase entry point. That evening he went into his bedroom and removed a heavy, metal toolbox from a cabinet. The toolbox had a hefty padlock on it that also tethered it, via a stout stainless steel chain, to an eyebolt he had anchored into the floor joist. He pulled his necklace out from inside his shirt and used the key on it to open the padlock. He removed a cloth bundle from the toolbox and carefully carried it up to the observation dome. He laid the bundle down on the oak table and gently unwrapped the cloth to reveal the jade figurine of Lauren that he had carved in Korea. He stood it in the center of the table and took a few steps back as the memories of carving it rushed through his mind. It was bittersweet, remembering the pain of being physically and mentally abused while also being touched by Shin's humanity and the comedy act of Young and Yong as they beat each other everyday over their game of mah-jong. He liked that the figurine finally had a home that matched the dignity with which he regarded it. He slept well that night and didn't wake up until 10:30 am the next morning.

CHAPTER 29

With a careless gesture, Gwon flicked his cigarette overboard and glanced at the luminous dial on his TechnoMarine XSMSH. While others might admire the amount of science represented by the sleek black timepiece, Gwon preferred the steel Submariner that normally encased his wrist. Soon, he assured himself, he would be out of the black turtleneck, back in the casually tailored linen that was his usual attire. Perhaps a visit to Koh Phangan, to enjoy the raucous parties and more sensual pleasures might be in order. There was always lovely company to be found near Hat Rin Nok.

He was briefly reminded of Lulu, the sweet little piece that had amused him in the past. Although he was well aware that her sparkling flattery was part of her trade, he also knew that she genuinely appreciated his smooth, muscled physique. How better to explain why, even after their first encounter, when he left her trembling and quivering in a ball, she sought him out the next night for another round, hissing away her competition like the alley cat that she was. Lulu, he was sure, was still about, and would be quite happy to se him— whatever else was true, he paid well for his diversions.

Dismissing such thoughts, he turned ot the business at hand. 10:07pm.

It was time.

He gave a small signal to the Zodiac's driver, who flipped a series of switches with practiced ease, finally pressing the red button that brought the Mercury outboards, with their six hundred horsepower, roaring to life. Gwon could feel the power behind the guttural rumble and popping of the tailpipes. He motioned the driver to pull away from the small dock, where they had been completely obscured from sight by a row of mangroves.

* * * * *

Michael Daniels knew these tiny, hidden bays dotted the edges of the western Pacific Ocean. He also knew they could hold creatures both quick and deadly. Some of these creatures were human. He gazed intently ahead, trying to see as far ahead as he could through the acrylic windows of the M/V *Malacca Queen's* bridge. More a floating city than a ship, the behemoth, weighing in at 130,000 tons, was one of the largest structures afloat, and was the pride of the Global Oil Fleet. The crew had taken on her load in Oman and had then stopped briefly in Sri Lanka, Burma, and Thailand, and still carried nearly all her crude as she began her run for California. It had been considered a huge honor when Daniels' eighteen years of faultless service had been rewarded with this post. On nights like this, it felt more like a curse.

The traffic in the Malacca Straits was heavy that night, and the light rain misting down further worsened the already low visibility. Hansen, the first officer, cleared his throat, and Captain Daniels was shaken out of his concentration.

"Sir, we're holding seven knots."

"Let's keep her steady."

Hansen looked rueful. "Steady as we can, Captain."

Despite her gargantuan size, the *Malacca Queen's* diesel engines could power her through the open ocean at speeds above twenty knots. But as they approached the more congested point in the straits, it was necessary to drop her speed as low as possible and still remain maneuverable.

"Radar?"

"The usual traffic. Some merchant vessels, fishing boats, probably some sampans out there." The fatigue and worry on

Hansen's face was evident. Everyone on the *Malacca Queen* knew the dangers that could lurk in this stretch of water.

"Well, let's hope the sampans will make way for us," Daniels said lightly.

Hansen chuckled in return. The sampans used by locals to carry their produce to the small markets across the straits were flimsy affairs constructed of wood and thatch. Their chances of colliding with one of the fast large ships that populated the straits were phenomenal, and still they ran, day and night.

However, the threat posed by the smaller vessels that choked the passage was not what chilled Daniels' blood. Though the ship he commanded resembled nothing so much as a floating fortress, Daniels knew that only a fool would feel himself secure. The darkness could easily conceal a threat against which the *Malacca Queen's* sheer bulk would prove useless.

* * * * *

Gwon's dark eyes narrowed as he examined the crate of weapons that had been opened for his inspection. After a sharp nod, the men on board quickly reached for the assault rifles, loading them with 7.62mm rounds and slipping extra magazines into their shoulder harnesses. Each man then armed himself with concussion grenades, a 9mm piston, and a small steel flashlight. Each man, except for Gwon. In a reflexive movement, his hand went to the Boker A-F578S combat knife that was sheathed at his side. That, and his forty-caliber Heckler-Koch model P7M10 pistol, were all that he would need.

As they rounded the point, the boat throttled forward, slid up to thirty knots and skipped lightly over the choppy waves of the strait proper. The night felt like warm black silk, and the spray coming over the bow sprayed each man's face with a taste of the salty Pacific.

* * * * *

As a boy, Daniels had loved Robert Louis Stevenson, and had dreamed of drama in the South Seas. Treasure maps, scarlet and vermilion parrots, eye patches, and tall-masted sailing schooners crewed by swashbuckling adventurers had filled his imagination. These things now seemed as quaint a a child's amusement park ride. The romantic relics of eighteenth-century maritime lore certainly bore no resemblance to the bands of criminals that were the real scourge of the South Seas.

Though the boy's mind had been rich with images of buried treasure, guarded by rum-soaked ghosts, by now the man had come face to face with the truth. Treasure was no longer buried, but floating, and he had accepted the near-impossible task of protecting it.

He had read dozens of reports of pirate encounters, and he personally knew two captains who had endured having their ships boarded. After listening to the accounts of the violence and chaos the attackers brought them, he agreed that both men were lucky to be around to tell their stories.

If a band made it aboard, Daniels had little recourse but to give the order to form the 'Citadel'. Under this order, the bridge and engineering spaces would be locked down to provide some modest protection for the crew. At that point the official policy was to let the pirates take whatever they wanted, and try to stay alive.

In the last three years, there had been a total of forty-two attacks on commercial vessels in the Malacca Straits alone. The oil companies had watched as their fleets sustained serious damage, and their revenues dipped, as pirate attacks became more frequent, and bolder. The satellite tracking systems attached to the ships had originally been used primarily to monitor how efficiently the tanker crews were delivering their million-dollar cargo. Increasingly, the satellites served to track the position of a ship that had been commandeered.

And maddeningly, in an age in which satellites could track a tanker's position within a yard's distance, Daniels and his fellow captains had almost no weapons with which to thwart an attack.

"Hansen, are all the floodlights positioned to maximum range?"

"Yes, Sir. And water cannons are at the ready."

"Good. Let's hope we don't' need them."

He had never tried to ward off a siege with the cannons, which were poised to drive back a potential assailant with 250 pounds of force. Furthermore, he had no wish to put the theoretical defense to the test.

Thought the *Malacca Queen* ran with floodlights bathing the deck and nearby water from sunset to sunrise, they did little more to discourage attacks than a lamp left on in an empty house. "We're watching you," the lights shouted in the night. "We can see what you're up to."

But Daniels knew it was an idle boast. A ship the size of the *Malacca Queen* had a radar system that tracked, with great accuracy, any vessels on the surface near them, but the transmitter for the radar was placed just ahead of the ship's funnel. This meant it could not scan the area astern of the ship, effectively creating a twenty-degree blind spot in the ship's defenses.

Though it had often been suggested that this deficiency could be remedied with an additional rearward-facing radar system, most ships, the *M/V Malacca Queen* had to take their chances without it. Right now, Daniels thought idly, they resembled nothing so much as an elephant trying to elude a wasp.

* * * * *

The signal on Gwon's handheld GPS showed the Zodiac's exact position, as well as a topographical map of the area that included ocean depth and tidal status. His tiny radar screen showed a sprinkling of blue dots— ships large and valuable enough to warrant such expensive satellite systems. Any one of the ships would have made a worthy target, but he ignored all but one, confirming that it was the *Malacca Queen*. He quickly ascertained the lack of a second radar system with a passive receiver.

Gwon knew that right now, any Captain worth his uniform would be anxiously scanning his surface radar, looking for any suspicious craft approaching at high speeds. But the *Malacca Queen's* flaw was Gwon's most powerful weapon. His cold gaze swept over the group in the boat. Not a twitch of fear showed in any face. There was no hesitation at being an instrument of death. Gwon had no doubt of who would emerge victorious from his fight with the steel Goliath.

At a silent signal, the men lowered their night-vision goggles, and waited calmly for the next order. After scanning the traffic in the straits, Gwon plotted a course that would bring the band directly up the center of the unguarded radar blind spot. Easily dodging several slower boats, the Zodiac closed in on its prey.

As Gwon had guessed, Daniels was, with practiced habit, scanning the radar screen every few seconds. SInce he knew it was perhaps the best hope he and his crew had of advanced warning of an attack, he had developed an uncanny ability to interpret even the slightest blip on the screen, discerning its size and speed at a glance.

He could quickly dismiss the generous radar return signatures of the metal-hulled merchant vessels. And sampans often gave no radar return, but if they did, it was almost always a slow-moving vessel meandering across the normal shipping lanes.

But among these electronic pulses that signified the blur of activity going on around the ship, Daniels saw something that made his heart skip a beat. A faint, almost indiscernible radar image showed a small craft moving with speed and purpose, directly toward the *Intrepid*. Daniels' eyes darted to the clock at the same time that Gwon casually checked his watch. 10:17.

CHAPTER 30

One of the items that had been left behind in Station 65 was a Draeger model BG-4AP self-contained respirator left by the fire fighters. He had not paid it much attention during the cleanup and renovation but now that things were more or less settled at Station 65, he decided to look at the unit more carefully. It had a full-face mask that connected to the main air tank and a backpack style harness for carrying it. He examined the valve body on the tank and quickly figured out how to turn it on. The valve had some slight corrosion on it but turned and let out the last little hiss of gas that still remained in the tank. Just out of curiosity he hefted the unit onto his back and pulled the mask over his face. The weight of the tank wasn't too bad and the mask felt comfortable. He walked around a little bit just to see what it must have been like to wear this unit while fighting a fire and concluded that if you're going to have to wear something like this it might as well be for SCUBA diving rather than firefighting. That got him to consider taking up a hobby in addition to his stone carving which he continued to do in the studio that he had outfitted in the observation dome.

Having no experience with SCUBA diving, he didn't know where to start so he asked Suzy at the diner if there was a dive shop around. She said that there was one in Raleigh and asked if he wanted her to go with him. He smiled slightly and declined the offer of her company and set off in the Range Rover.

At the Ridgeway Aquatic Dive Shop in Raleigh he examined the extensive selection of dive gear available. The shop's owner saw his perplexed look and offered his services in helping Connelly pick out some gear. They spent an hour or so looking over the various options as the shop owner had to explain a lot. In the end, Connelly had him assemble a dive gear package consisting of the finest gear available. When he was at the register the shop owner totaled everything up and looked at Connelly.

"OK, and let me see your PADI card," the shop owner said.

Connelly paused for a moment and calculated.

"I don't have one right now," he said.

The shop owner's chest sunk as he felt a seven-thousand dollar sale slipping away.

"Well, legally, I can't sell you this equipment if you're not certified by one of the sanctioned diving agencies," he replied.

Connelly looked down at the sales counter and scanned the various advertisements displayed there. He pointed to a handwritten page.

"I see here that you give dive classes every other month," Connelly said.

"That's right, we teach the classes right near here. It's about thirty hours of instruction and you get certified when we take the open water dive at Fantasy Lake," he explained.

Connelly's fingers slid over to the total on his receipt.

"I tell you what- let me buy this gear and I'll promise to sign up for your next class- we'll say that I'm conducting pre-dive equipment familiarization. In the meantime I'll study these books and be book-ready when the time comes for the lessons," he offered.

The shop owner decided that his offer was sufficient to allow the controversial transaction to take place and give him enough profit to close the shop for the rest of the week.

"That'll work, Mister Connelly," he happily agreed.

They completed the transaction and the shop owner helped him get the gear into his Range Rover.

"Thanks again and I'll see you at the first lesson," Connelly said.

The shop owner smiled, waved, and headed back into the shop which was closed five minutes later.

When Connelly got back to Station 65, he unloaded all of the equipment and carried it into one of the auxiliary rooms on the ground floor where he laid it out in a meaningful way on the floor. He spent two days studying the intricacies of the buoyancy compensator, the primary and secondary stages of the regulator, the dive tables, dive computer, and the hazards of embolism and nitrogen-narcosis. It was a lot of information to absorb but he had developed a tremendous ability to focus on a task and study it until he completely understood it. Then he read the dive guides from cover-to-cover and completed the quizzes in each chapter with one-hundred percent correct answers. He tried on the gear, including the full wetsuit and fins. He breathed through the regulator for five minutes and felt quite comfortable with its operation. He felt that he knew how to dive.

CHAPTER 31

The seasoned attackers hunkered down inside the boat, coiled like cobras ready to strike. The pilot had, at this point, gotten a clear view of the target ship. He kept the attack boat at full speed until the last possible moment when he suddenly slammed the throttles into the full-reverse position, causing the propellers to twist under the torque of suddenly slowing the boat to match the *M/V Malacca Queen's* seven knots.

Captain Daniels, of course, heard nothing on the bridge. Even if the acrylic windows weren't good acoustic insulation, it would be difficult to hear an attack boat over the white noise generated by the ship's hull in the water. His own diesel engines could easily drown out the noise of a modern traffic jam. Insulated in his cocoon on the bridge, he was unaware that his perimeter defenses were being penetrated.

"Foomp!" was the muted sound that came from the grappling cannon. The sound came again as Gwon directed another hook to be fired. With the attack boat positioned against the tanker's stern it was easy to use the hand-held cannons to lob a three-pronged grappling hook over the ship's transom and secure it for climbing. Within seconds, two polypropylene lines had been hung from the tanker and the pirates were ascending the lines.

Gwon reached the transom and deftly sprung over the steel wall and landed gently on the steel deck. He immediately drew his P7M10 and slipped a few feet away to take cover behind a winch drum. The three others had assumed a standard fire-support formation on the deck.

Captain Daniels' gut started to tighten.

"Where's that speedboat?" he barked out to no one in particular. Hansen was the only other person on the bridge and, as such, felt obliged to reply.

"I don't know, Captain. I'll ask the sentries."

Hansen pulled a hand-held transceiver from his pocket and walked over to the bridgewing. Looking down onto the aft starboard section of the weather deck, he pressed the transmit button.

"Arun, come in."

On the deck, Arun, a hired Malaysian crewman, snapped out of his light nap at the sound of the Hansen's voice on the transceiver. Normally he wouldn't have responded to a radio call but he knew that two people on the crew could withhold his pay if he screwed up and Hansen was one of them.

"Arun here," he responded with fabricated seriousness.

"Do you see a speedboat anywhere off the stern?"

Arun took a quick glance over the side and didn't see anything.

"No, it's clear over here," he replied, belying the lack of effort he had exerted. He didn't realize Commander Hansen was watching him from the bridgewing overhead. However, the XO was inquiring mostly to calm the captain and felt no need to reprimand the lackadaisical crewman at this time.

"The sentry reports clear, Captain," Hansen reported.

Daniels didn't respond and took a deep breath as he scrutinized the radar screen image. He was sure he had seen a high-speed target approaching them and had not seen it move away. His gut tightened a bit more.

Arun had not seen the attack boat which was now keeping station twenty yards off the tanker's stern. Neither did he see Ahn as the pirate silently moved in behind the slack crewman. In one swift motion the black-clad boarder hooked his leg around Arun's so he couldn't move, pulled his chin up with dizzying force, and slashed his throat with unquestioned force and speed. The blood stains were unnoticeable on Ahn's black jumpsuit and only slightly more visible on the deck. He took the body of his victim and maneuvered it over a few feet against the gunwale so it wouldn't be seen right away.

Gwon and one other pirate moved forward around the starboard side of the wheelhouse while the other pair made their way around the port side.

"Ask the sentry again if he sees anything," Daniels ordered with growing severity.

Hansen brought the transceiver to his mouth and asked Arun if he saw anything. There was no response.

"Damn, that guy's a lazy bum," Hansen muttered under his breath. He tried again. Daniels noticed the lack of response and began to stand up straight as he ordered the XO to query a sentry on the port side.

"Som, this is the XO. Do you see anything off the stern?"

Like before, there was no response. Hansen had thought the hired hands were just slack but he was now beginning to share some of the captain's concern. What Hansen didn't know was that the reason his port side sentry wasn't responding was that he too was lying on the deck lifeless.

"Stern port clear," called one of the pirates into his headset microphone.

"Take the wheelhouse and secure the captain," Gwon ordered.

As the port side pair ascended the ladders to the bridge, Gwon and his partner made their way forward to a hatch that led down into the ship. They quickly slid down the stair rails and made their way down a dimly lit corridor.

Daniels, fully alert now, gave the order for the ship to be locked down.

"This is the captain. We are now at condition S-1. Form the Citadel," he ordered with clarity and conviction.

Hansen immediately locked the hatches to the bridge and secured the latches on the windows. He pulled his binoculars up to his eyes to survey the deck and make sure the crew was performing the Citadel checklist.

"Bring us to four knots and keep her steady," the captain whispered to Hansen.

The captain quickly turned and hustled down the ladder from the bridge into the main corridor. He ran to the port hatch and slipped a padlock through the lever. He likewise secured the starboard hatch then proceeded to run to his cabin. Once inside he calmly but quickly opened the safe and pulled out a satchel with $10,000 cash in it. He kept this satchel in his cabin at all times in the even of a boarding. From his conversations with other captains he had learned that pirates could often be placated with cash and it usually took a five-figure sum to do it. Given that Daniels was now making more than ten times that each year, he felt it was a reasonable insurance policy to carry.

He grasped the satchel's handle tightly as he sprinted back up the corridor towards the bridge. When he arrived at the bottom of the stairs that led back into the bridge he stopped. He felt something was very wrong and had that feeling confirmed when he saw Hansen's hand hanging limp over the edge of the stairwell. He could tell it was Hansen's hand since the wristwatch attached to it was the Tag Huer that Daniels had given him last Christmas. Daniels stood frozen trying to remain silent. His camouflage was blown when he saw the whites of a pair of eyes looking down from the bridge. The black nylon cap was an instant indication that this man was not a crewmember.

Daniels sprinted down the corridor as the attacker quickly slid down the stairwell. By the time he had made the bottom of the stairs, however, Daniels had slipped through a hatch and secured it behind him. He took a fire extinguisher from the wall and jammed it into the hatch's lever so that it couldn't be opened. He had seen this in a training video that was emphasizing the dangers of improperly secured items onboard a ship. This was one misplacement that was going to extend his life span. Within seconds the pirate had made it to the door and struggled to open the lever. From the other side it was impossible to get enough leverage on the handle to dislodge or crush the extinguisher. Quickly he realized the captain had gotten away.

"Alpha is headed south," the pirate calmly called into his microphone.

Gwon acknowledged the report indicating that the captain was headed towards the engineering spaces of the ship. He was in the middle of disabling the diesel injector pump when the call came but realized that 'Alpha' was more important. He quietly but quickly moved back across Engineering to the point where Daniels was most likely to appear. Gwon had committed a detailed map of the interior of the ship to his memory so that it wouldn't slow him down in these unexpected situations.

Running down another hallway, Daniels' mind raced in an effort to formulate a plan to save his life. He knew that the ship had been commandeered and probably most of the crew had been killed. He couldn't retake the bridge by himself so the ship's fate was largely out of his hands. He now focused on his own life. He was startled by the sound of footsteps approaching him and he quickly looked around for a place to hide but didn't have time before the man saw him. Luckily, it was a Filipino crewman who looked even more frightened than himself.

"Which way?" the desperate crewman asked in broken English.

"This way!" Daniels replied with far more confidence than he actually possessed.

The two of them ran down the corridor towards Engineering. Daniels figured that the best way to survive would be to find a dark corner and wait it out. Hopefully the pirates would disembark and he could retake the ship before it hit another ship or foundered in the straits.

On the bridge, the pair of pirates were guiding the ship with expert care. They had resumed the standard seven-knot speed dictated by Hughes Consolidated's operations manual and had even made two radio calls to other tankers who were straying slightly off-course. To all outward appearances the M/V *Malacca Queen* was still under the control of its seasoned crew.

"Two, this is Lead. Status," Gwon whispered into his microphone.

"We're five-by-five in the channel. Bridge secure, speed and course stable."

No other communication was made as Gwon could hear the approach of two people. He silently slipped the Boker A-F578S from its scabbard and gripped it tightly, having already put his pistol back in its holster.

Daniels and the Filipino reached the end of the corridor and were faced with a fork in the hallway. He motioned for the crewman to go to the right, knowing that there were a number of small compartments in which the small man could hide. The Filipino responded with a quick nod, understanding what the captain meant for him to do. Daniels turned to the left and headed off in search of his own quiet, dark corner but he would never make it.

CHAPTER 32

The next morning Connelly packed everything into the Range Rover, including the two extra tanks he had purchased and had filled at the dive shop. He followed Highway 15 up to Kerr Lake and spent a half-hour finding a secluded perch that would allow easy access into the lake. It took him thirty minutes to don the suit and get the buoyancy compensator settled on his back. He adjusted the tank just as the dive guide had instructed and became familiar with the location of the controls and the position of his tank pressure gauge and the dive computer so that he could find them without looking.

He found a spot on the shoreline where a rock ledge overhung the water surface about three feet up. He made sure that there was an easy egress point nearby so that he could get out later with the fifty or so pounds of gear on. The rock ledge allowed him a way to ingress into the water without stumbling around in his fins and risking falling down. He inflated his buoyancy compensator (BC) to its maximum level, bulging out around his chest to provide positive buoyancy. He made sure the regulator was providing air and he held his mask to his face as he took a split-step and fell into the water.

On the initial entry, he sank a few feet and then began to rise to the surface. His breathing accelerated rapidly as the sensation of submerging caused a natural panic reaction. After a few seconds and many rapid breaths, his aspiration returned to a normal rate and he bobbed up and down gently at the surface of the lake. The cold water on his hands and cheeks told him that the lake would punish anyone without a dive suit almost instantaneously with hypothermia. However, the six point five-millimeter Akona suit was keeping his torso, arms, and legs nice and warm and he felt comfortable. So far, everything was going great and he had followed all of the rules, except the most important one- never dive alone. He had considered this in great depth and had concluded that he wasn't ready to take on someone in that capacity and that diving couldn't be that hard or dangerous.

He checked his regulator twice and the amount of pressure in his tank, which read 3,000 psi, which was full. He pulled on the ribbed hose on his left shoulder which let air out of the buoyancy compensator and he began to descend. The sound of his breathing dominated his attention but the pressure building on his ear drums quickly got his attention. Being an experienced pilot he was able to quickly and easily equalize the pressure in his ears and continue descending.

Having studied the dive table extensively, he had decided that this first dive would be down to fifty feet and he would stay twenty-five minutes. Under these conditions he would not need to perform a 'decompression stop' on the return ascent to purge built-up nitrogen from his bloodstream. His only constraint on the ascent would be speed, knowing that ascending too fast will cause the air in his bloodstream to form a bubble and cause a deadly embolism.

After a few minutes, his wrist-mounted altimeter indicated a depth of fifty feet and he arrested his descent by pressing the button on the ribbed hose which transferred compressed air from his tank into the buoyancy compensator. Making a few adjustments to get his buoyancy neutral, Connelly was quite satisfied with the state of his dive. On the descent he had concentrated on breathing properly and clearing his ears while he watched the depth. The timer on the dive gauge had started and he now had twenty-two minutes left for his no-decompression dive.

He looked around and could see some features on the steeply-angled shoreline. The sunlight was significantly dimmer at this depth but still allowed identification of major shapes. The lake bed wall was mostly rock but had some green-plant growth on it. He rotated his body into a horizontal position and gently thrust his fins up and down to propel himself towards the wall. He examined the rocks, noting how they were slightly different under the surface than above. The features of the algae-like growths on the wall were hard to distinguish so he retrieved his dive light from the clip on his belt and used it to illuminate the plant life. He spent a few minutes looking around and absorbing the sensations of this alien environment. He was surprised at how well he could hear various events in the lake, like a gentle waterfall somewhere and some occasional fish jumping around making audible sounds. The weightless sensation felt great as it relieved his legs and joints of the normal stress put on them by gravity. It was comfortable and felt very free. He consulted his dive watch - seventeen minutes left and 2,400 psi.

He turned around and kicked his fins casually a few times to look around. He spent a few minutes swimming about and noticing how difficult it was to see very far. There were various light and dark regions but not much detail. After a few minutes, though, something caught his eye. Down below he saw a lighter shape that had a couple of sparkly points on it. He was intrigued. He turned his dive light toward the object and could tell that it was not natural. It did not look like a rock formation or a clump of submerged trees. It was something man-made. He pulled the compensator hose to release some air and began a gentle descent towards the mysterious object. As he got closer he could see that it was at least partially metallic although severely corroded. When he got within ten feet of it he realized that it was a vehicle of some kind that had settled on the bottom of the lake. As he scanned over the hull he had to fight his buoyancy a little bit to stay at his new depth. Once he got the setting right on his compensator he moved towards the object. He noticed a large, flat section that had been torn off, leaving a ragged edge and that was attached to a vertical piece that had a... canopy. It was an airplane! Connelly's pulse jumped up as he realized that he had encountered a sunken plane. A quick examination showed it to be a World War II era fighter plane, probably a dive-bomber. He figured that it must have crashed during a training flight since there was a lot of training done at various airfields in that part of the country during the war. He swam around the tail of the aircraft, noting the US Navy insignia on the empenage. He made his way forward and looked into the cockpit, seeing a tattered leather flight jacket and a pair of boots. He somberly realized that this poor guy didn't get out and probably drowned to death. His own ejection from his U-2 flashed through his mind as he contemplated the horrible scene of this plane crashing. He tried to read the name on the jacket but it was far too deteriorated. After a silent memorial for the fallen aviator, he slipped around the front of the aircraft to look at the engine for signs of what caused the crash. The engine seemed more or less intact and didn't show any signs of fire as best as he could tell. Maybe he ran out of gas or flew into bad weather and didn't know how to fly out of it. Whatever happened, it wasn't a pleasant way to go for sure.

Connelly's fantasizing about what happened to cause this crash was interrupted by a faint red flashing. He looked around and realized it was coming from his dive computer! He spun his wrist over and was horrified to see that he had exceeded his twenty-five minute dive time by nine minutes! 'Oh shit!' he muttered into his regulator as he realized that he would have to perform a decompression stop. In a second he also realized that he had descended further than planned... eighty-two feet! 'Oh fuck!' he thought as he considered that he had blown both his depth and time significantly. Without the dive tables he had no idea had long his decompression stop would need to be. He spent thirty second calming himself as he struggled to remember to dive table's numbers. 'I can just be on the conservative side, that's all' he thought to himself. 'I'll take a nice, long deco stop at fifty feet and then another nice, long one at twenty feet before I surface. That'll get the nitrogen out of my bloodstream,' he thought. He then considered that he been down for a fairly long time at a significant depth, doing a lot of strenuous swimming, all factors that increase the rate of air use out of his precious tank. He slowly grasped the tank gauge and rolled the dial into sight, hoping that if he snuck up on it, it might somehow not be down very far.

Seven-hundred psi. 'Shit'. Yellow zone on the gauge, only two-hundred psi above the red zone. He pressed the inflate button on the regulator to begin his ascent. He immediately shuddered when he realized that he had just taken some breathable air out of his tank. 'Dammit!'. Six hundred psi.

The ubiquitous warnings about embolism from a rapid ascent flashed in his mind. His dive watch calculated his ascent and he forced himself to stay below the maximum recommended safe ascent rate. As he rose through seventy feet and then sixty feet he considered the decompression stop carefully. He didn't remember where the optimum decompression depth was so he decided that he'd stop at twenty-five feet and stay there as long as he could before surfacing.

When he reached twenty-five feet he blew some of the precious air out of his compensator so that he would maintain his depth. He grasped the air gauge. One-hundred-fifty psi. 'I might be fucked,' he thought. He consciously forced himself to calm down and breath slowly as his blood rid itself of the excess nitrogen. During those calm few minutes the irony of the situation struck him. If he died during this dive, he would have killed himself in a totally voluntary act of leisure having survived almost two years in a POW camp after bailing out of his jet. That would be very, very embarrassing.

He kept an eye on his gauge and could feel each breath coming with more and more effort, his lungs straining to pull the last of the gas from the tank as the needle crept down to zero. When he felt he couldn't drag any more air from the tank, he filled his lungs and then exhaled into the manual-fill valve on the compensator to initiate an ascent. This served a second purpose, vacating the air from his lungs and thus preventing an embolism. As he kicked his legs he could feel the stinging in his empty lungs. The surface was near but he could hardly see it. He pushed and pushed and finally breached the surface.

His first lungful was precious life, but the second included a large dose of water that caused him to cough and gag for several minutes as he struggled to keep his head above the surface and get air into his deprived lungs. He finally managed a stable position on the surface and cleared his head enough to look around and realize that he had drifted three hundred yards from his entry point and the place where he had identified an easy egress route. His arms felt like lead-filled bags and his legs were almost useless. The nitrogen in his bloodstream was seriously depriving his muscles of oxygen and they didn't perform well.

He struggled, paddling with his weary arms, and made it to the edge of the lake in twenty minutes. It took another ten minutes to find a place where he could drag himself out of the water. He immediately popped the clasp on his tank harness and rolled out onto his back. As he stared up into the sun it felt like a truck had deposited a load of sand onto his chest and legs. It would take forty-five minutes before the effects of nitrogen loading wore off enough so that he could drag his gear back to the Range Rover and climb in.

Feeling a bit disoriented, he went directly to Benson's, sat at the counter, and was immediately delivered his usual coffee by Suzy. He gripped the cup with both hands and gently sipped it. Suzy noticed that his hair was a bit wet and looked at his

Range Rover parked immediately outside. She saw the SCUBA gear through the window and quickly figured out what he had been doing that afternoon. Her eyes darted quickly between his eyes and his coffee cup, which she was refilling although he had only had time to take two sips from it.

"Did some SCUBA diving, huh?" she asked.

Connelly looked up at her and answered her with a couple of quick nods.

"You know, Dixie is an experienced diver," she offered hesitantly.

"Who's Dixie?"

Suzy's eyes lit up with surprise and fondness.

"Oh, you don't know Dixie? He's great. He runs the airfield just south of town."

"I didn't know there was an airport near here," Connelly confessed.

"Oh yeah, it's about fifteen minutes out of town on Highway 15." she said as she swept her hair behind her right ear. "You should go visit him; he's real nice... an older black fella that used to fly airplanes for the weather channel or something. He teaches skydiving and flying and stuff now but he's mostly retired and just hangs out. He owns the airport and has a small place attached to it where he lives. I'm sure he'd like to meet you."

Connelly spent the next hour sipping coffee and reviewing in his head what had happened. He silently cursed himself several times for being so stupid. Eventually he settled down and thought more about this 'Dixie' person that Suzy had mentioned and thought that he sounded interesting.

Connelly went to bed early that evening and slept soundly. He awoke at his usual 5:00am the next morning and took his cup of coffee up into the observation dome where he wrapped a wool blanket around himself as he sat in an armchair that he had recently moved up there. In the short time he had been living at Station 65 he had grown to really appreciate the early morning view from this vantage point. He could see the gorgeous mountains and the lake nearby as well as miles and miles of verdant forest. The sunrises were spectacular and the sunsets glorious from this perch and he tried to never miss one.

As he was finishing his coffee he noticed a small plane flying south and wondered if it was heading to Dixie's airport. He decided to find out.

The drive down Highway 15 took about fifteen minutes, as Suzy had reliably described. The small green sign with the icon of an airplane indicated where he needed to turn off and he found a fairly narrow gravel road that led through a quarter mile or so of trees before opening up to the small airport. There was one hangar of moderate size and several other smaller ones. The large hangar had a small structure attached to it that could easily be the residence of Dixie as Suzy described. Connelly found a small parking lot where an old pickup truck stood alone. He pulled the Rover in next to the pickup and pulled on his warm L.L. Bean coat as he stepped out onto the gravel lot. He walked onto the ramp and could see that the runway was paved and remarkably long for the size of the airport- he estimated it was 4,000 feet in length, long enough to bring in a small business jet.

He walked around the ramp, taking stock of the aircraft that lived there. A half-dozen Cessna 172s and Piper Warriors populated the ramp along with a pair of home-built kit planes. He cautiously strolled across the ramp towards the hangars and noticed that the large hangar housed three aircraft, two older twin-engine Beechcraft Barons and a DeHavilland Twin Otter. He walked slowly towards the hangar, looking carefully to see if anyone was around. He called out a couple of times but got no response and entered the hangar cautiously. He walked slowly towards the Otter and stopped about ten feet away from it. He looked at it, stared at it even, and imagined what it sounded like with the Pratt and Whitney turboprop engines whining at full power and the air rushing past the nose cone. He thought back to his days learning to fly the T-2 Buckeye trainer in the Navy and how he looked at the T-2 the same way the first time he saw it. After several minutes he closed the distance and stood immediately next to the nose of the Otter. He gently put his hand out and touched the painted surface as a child might touch a pony for the first time. The physical connection seemed to open a conduit for him, a pathway into his past as a pilot.

"You must be a pilot," a voice called out, startling Connelly. He quickly withdrew his hand and shot it back into his coat pocket.

"I'm sorry. I didn't know anyone was here," Connelly replied.

The man was standing at a doorway inside the hangar, leaning against the doorframe with his hands in his pockets.

"You must be Dixie," Connelly said.

"That's right. And I'm figuring you must be Connelly."

Connelly squinted his eyes as Dixie slowly walked over to him.

"Oh, Stovall's not that big so it wasn't much of a guess. Somebody comes to town, takes over Station 65 and hangs out at Benson's... that makes the local gossip pretty quickly. I'm Dixie Walker and it's a pleasure to meet," he said as he stuck out his hand and shook Connelly's.

"I'm sorry about just walking in your hangar. Suzy told me about your place here and I... just wanted to see it."

"Like I said- you must be a pilot," Dixie replied.

"What makes you think I'm a pilot?"

"People who aren't pilots don't just visit small airports. And I can also tell by the way you were touching the nose of the Otter- that's not a casual gesture."

Connelly only nodded slowly in response.

"Suzy tells me that you are a SCUBA diver," Connelly said, abruptly changing he subject.

"That's right. I used to dive a lot when I first started working for NOAA."

"What else did you do for the Administration?" Connelly asked.

"Well, I dove for a year or so until they found out that I used to fly turboprops for a freight hauler. It just so happened that they needed a flight engineer for a new aircraft and I fit the bill. Eventually I worked my way into the pilot's seat and flew hurricane missions for sixteen years."

"Hurricane hunter? Fascinating!" Connelly replied.

"So, what did you do before you returned to Stovall?" Dixie asked.

"What do you mean, 'returned'?" Connelly coyly asked.

"Like I said, AJ, news travels fast in Stovall."

"So you probably know what I did," Connelly said.

"I heard you were in the Navy, but that's all anybody seems to know."

"Well, yes, I was in the Navy and I did Navy things, mostly paperwork. I spent some time in intelligence gathering and analysis. Nothing exciting."

Dixie nodded a few time with a grin on his face.

"OK, Mister Connelly, that's fine. So, do you want to go diving some time?"

"Yes, I did. Uh, I would." He swallowed hard and then proceeded to tell Dixie about what had happened that morning.

"Ah, you found the old Avenger! I've dove on that wreck several times. Really sad about Blalock. His grandkids live in Raleigh but they hate to talk about the wreck. Anyway, why don't we plan a dive and do it by the book?"

"Sounds great. When would you like to go?"

"How about tomorrow morning?" Dixie quickly replied.

The next morning Connelly met Dixie at the airport and loaded his gear into the back of the Rover and drove to the lake. Dixie's dive computer was older but worked just fine as they enjoyed a properly executed dive on the Avenger. Dixie pointed out a number of noteworthy markings on the plane, identifying its squadron and vintage. Before and after the dive, he gave Connelly the detailed history of how the young pilot had become disoriented in the clouds, getting caught in a sudden storm that dropped in on the training flight. His flight leader tried to talk him out of the predicament but he panicked for just a few seconds and nosed the plane over into an unrecoverable dive. He probably survived the impact with the surface of the water but drowned, another victim of the unforgiving nature of aviation towards mistakes.

Over the next three months Dixie and Connelly dove at various spots in North Carolina, going to the coast and ocean diving twice. Dixie was a patient and excellent dive instructor and never once questioned Connelly about diving with no training. They spent some time together at Benson's talking about all kinds of things but managing to avoid discussing in detail Connelly's days in the Navy related to his crash. Dixie got the sense that much of what Connelly had done was classified and knew to not pry too much.

One afternoon, Connelly showed up at the airport to pick up Dixie just as an unpredicted storm rolled in. The two sat in the main hangar next to the Otter for a couple of hours, trying to wait out the storm. Eventually Dixie sat down in front of his Intel iMac and pulled up a web site that was used for internal NOAA purposes only.

"How come I've never seen this web page?" Connelly asked.

"Well, the general public doesn't have access to it. I still know some guys at the Administration and they let me log in."

They sifted through the various meteorological data pages and concluded that the storm was going to last for several hours and they decided to cancel their diving for that day. They strolled back into the main hangar and sat in a couple of chairs at a maintenance desk.

"Well, there's really one thing to do on a day like this," Dixie said as he pulled a bottle of wine from the bottom drawer. Connelly smiled broadly at the gesture.

"I haven't drunk anything in years," Connelly confessed.

"Moral objection?" Dixie queried.

"No... no reason really!"

"Well then, let's update your drinking status," Dixie said as he pulled the cork out of a bottle of 1997 Jordan Wineries cabernet sauvignon and poured two coffee mugs full. Connelly didn't know much about wines but could tell that this was good stuff. He hadn't drunk anything since before Korea so the alcohol got to him fast. They continued drinking and talking for hours until the sun had gone down along with Connelly's inhibitions.

"So, AJ, you never answered my question," Dixie said.

"What question is that?"

"The very first question I ever asked you. Are you a pilot?"

Connelly looked down into his mug of red wine and inhaled deeply, the vapors coaxing his past out of him.

"Yeah, I was a pilot," he said as he took a long draw on the wine.

"I figured. What did you fly?"

"The Dragon Lady."

Dixie's eyebrows raised up as he recognized the nickname of the U-2. Suddenly, a lot of things fell into place about Connelly's secretive nature.

"That's quite a ride," Dixie said.

"Yes, it sure was... and the view from 75,000 feet is just spectacular. There were days when I thought that lady would keep climbing and take me into orbit. Such a gorgeous plane..."

Dixie's voice softened as he continued.

"How long did you fly the U-2?"

"Forty-three takeoffs, forty-two landings," was the cryptic answer.

"I heard that's a real tough bird to fly. Lots of folks, good pilots, landed those things shiny-side down."

"Yeah, but how many got hit by a missile over Korea?" he blurted as he took another long swig from the mug.

Dixie did not answer, knowing that Connelly had just laid out a huge part of his past. They sat in silence for another fifteen minutes as Connelly went over parts of the experience in his head and Dixie left him alone to process the memories. A few minutes later Connelly's eyelids bounced together as he fought to stay awake but was losing the fight. The mug, empty now, fell harmlessly onto a pile of rags as Connelly slumped forward in the chair, already snoring. Dixie grabbed his shoulders and guided him down onto some flattened cardboard boxes and covered him with a relatively clean fabric windshield cover. He waited for twenty minutes or so to make sure Connelly would be OK and then he took himself to his bedroom in the attached building and crashed for the night himself.

CHAPTER 33

The image of a large oil tanker hovered behind the newscaster's face as she read the latest headline from the wire.

"The 150,000 ton oil tanker *Malacca Queen* was found adrift this morning after its owners informed the U.S. Navy that it had lost communication with the ship. Its onboard GPS system, tracking the ship's progress, indicated that it had strayed off course at about the same time communication was lost. The Navy has not made an official statement regarding the rescue operation but inside sources are saying that the crew was killed and or captured. No motive had been established for the hijacking but it is estimated that the crew carried thousands of dollars in cash and that may have been the motive."

"Exactly $37,000, Miss Deborah Brown of CNN," Gwon whispered through his clenched teeth as he and his pirate band stored the cash they had stolen from the crew members and the captain's safe. The money, mostly American dollars, was safely stored in watertight ammo boxes and locked to rings in the floorboard of the Zodiac where six other boxes had already been secured. There was space for many, many more.

CHAPTER 34

Over the course of the next year Connelly and Dixie went diving several times a month and built a friendship over dinners and the occasional bottle of good red wine. Connelly had settled in and become a member of the Stovall community, even participating in the annual fair by donating some stone carvings for the auction. He was almost a fixture at Benson's and had become trusted friends with Suzy even if that was her second choice for what kind of relationship she'd like to have with him. He kept a low profile for the most part, spending most of his time at Station 65 or conducting small dive excursions to one of the many lakes in North Carolina and southern Virginia. He and Dixie had made several ocean dives, which were more challenging, but offered a greater expanse and diversity to explore. Connelly hoped that they would do more ocean diving in the coming years.

During that same year Gwon and his band of pirates stayed very busy. Their bravado increased in proportion to their prowess at the art of the hijack. Driven by the passion to complete his goal as set forth by General Seong, Gwon kept a long-burning focus on building up his cash reserves to eventually have enough to buy the weapon from the Iranian conspirators. He also needed a vessel to complete the final strike in the mission and he was learning about ships and their abilities each time he commandeered one. The day would come, soon he hoped, when he would have enough resources the take his people to glory.

CHAPTER 35

Connelly awoke on another one of North Carolina's splendid, gorgeous May mornings. A crisp pine scent floated through Station 65 and the chirping of the blue jays outside completed the Norman Rockwell-like moment. He got his cup of coffee and headed up into the observation dome as he usually did.

The previous week he had finished a gorgeous sandstone carving of a stalking panther and even stained it black for effect. Suzy's birthday was coming up and he thought she might like to have this piece and, besides, the shelf space in the observation dome was getting scarce as his carving skills led to a prolific production habit. He looked at the figurine of Lauren sitting on its special table and decided that another carving from jade would be just right. He rarely worked in jade since it was difficult to carve and quite expensive- no mines to pluck it from in Stovall.

He decided to make a rendering of Dixie's Twin Otter and started in on the project with as much enthusiasm as you could bear on a patient craft such as stone carving.

Down at Benson's, Dixie was finishing his late-afternoon cup of coffee when he felt a knot form in his stomach. He had been around long enough to know when something meant trouble and the brunette at the counter set off the alarms in Dixie's head. He quietly paid for his coffee and left Suzy a generous tip as he always did.

He managed to discreetly exit the diner and even keep a low profile as he started the four-hundred-twenty-seven cubic inch motor in his 1968 Camaro. He slid the car out of the parking space and crept away from Benson's.

Connelly's ears perked up when the Camaro was still a good five hundred yards away. Over the years he had learned the sound of Dixie's muscle car and could identify it at a great distance. It was unusual, however, for Dixie to drive up to Station 65 unexpectedly. Connelly sipped his tea as he watched the dark green car gently roll down his driveway and stop by the roll-up door.

Connelly opened the front door and let Dixie in without a word. He took another sip from his tea and set the cup on the counter as he and Dixie sat down on the bar stools. Dixie looked down for a few seconds before he spoke.

"Connelly, I know you were in the Navy and did some pretty serious stuff. I don't know what all you actually did and I don't really want to know." He paused for a few seconds before continuing. "I worked for the government long enough to know one when I see one and I saw one today. Down at Benson's there was a lady, quite attractive I'd say, wearing a charcoal gray suit with a brown briefcase. She was driving a dark green Taurus with blackwall tires and no markings of any kind. She was put together real well, spit and polish and all that," he described.

"OK, so what's got you so spooked about her?" Connelly asked.

"A combination of two things got me worried. One, she ain't from Stovall. Two, she was asking about you."

Connelly got a cool rush through his fingers and toes. His mind raced as he tried to guess who she was and why she was there. Of course, the first person that popped into his mind was Jurgensen and Connelly figured that he had decided to terminate their agreement and send this brunette to deliver the news. The thing that bothered him was that Jurgensen's style would be more subtle, like simply terminating the monthly payments and then not answering his phone. It was an awful lot of effort to send someone hunting around North Carolina to find him and tell him in person. It gnawed at him.

"Yeah, well, I knew this day would come sooner or later. Can't hide in the woods forever before the government decides to screw things up for you," he said as he picked up his cup and took a sip of tea. The two men sat in silence for a minute as each contemplated the situation.

"Listen, AJ, she smells like trouble to me. If you want to stay at the airport for a few days you're welcome to it. Or we can take that diving trip to the Bahamas like we've been talking about - I can have the Otter airborne in fifteen. What do you say we pack up and get the hell out of here for a week?"

"Thanks, Dixie, I really appreciate that and it sounds very, very tempting. But, whoever this is, she's gonna follow me around until she finds me. No doubt she'll turn Stovall upside down and piss off everybody here until we come back," he said. Then, after pausing for a few seconds he continued. "Besides, I'll have to deal with whatever this is sooner or later."

"OK, it's your call but I'll be at the airport all night. My schedule is clear tomorrow so I'll stay close by in case you change your mind. Just remember that we can be off the ground a few minutes after you decide to go."

He gave Connelly a pat on the shoulder as he got up and made for the door.

"Thanks, Dixie."

Connelly didn't sleep well that night and woke up earlier than usual. He went up to the observation dome and looked at the predawn sky and traced out the constellations he knew. The air was particularly clear that morning and the expanse of stars open to his view was stunning. He made a cup of coffee and just sat in the dome, not in the mood to do any carving. He went over the time he spent in Korea in his mind and how things had changed during the time he had been living in Stovall. He liked how things had progressed and even his brother Dan felt more comfortable with Connelly's disposition after spending the previous Thanksgiving together. Everything was settled and life, although a bit lean, was pleasurable and relaxing... until now.

An hour later, when the first morning light struck the driveway leading to Station 65, Connelly heard the sound of car tires. He opened the hatch on the observation dome and stepped out onto the roof of the station. He discreetly walked to a position on the roof where he could see down onto the driveway but it was difficult for people on the ground to see him because of the trees behind him.

A dark green Taurus, just as Dixie had described, pulled up to the station slowly and stopped. It took about three minutes for the occupant to appear from the car and she too was just as Dixie had described: a well proportioned women with dark hair pulled into a ponytail wearing a very nice dark gray skirt suit with plain, one inch heels and carrying a government-issued briefcase. He couldn't see her face well from his vantage point but he could tell that she was quite attractive. She adjusted her suit and brushed some imaginary debris off of her briefcase. She squared her shoulders and walked slowly towards the front door of the station. He listened carefully but couldn't hear the sound of knocking. After a full minute he saw the woman walking briskly back towards her car. She opened the door and tossed her briefcase into the passenger's seat. She started to get in but stopped herself. After a few deep breaths and a minute to recompose herself she walked resolutely to the door and knocked firmly on the door. Connelly debated answering the door but decided to get it over with. He went back into the dome and walked slowly down the stairs and into the foyer where the door was.

Connelly opened the door and stared at the woman standing in front of him. It was Lauren. His heart began racing faster than he could ever remember it going and his toes and fingers ran cold. After a second to confirm his identity, a broad smile broke across Lauren's face and then disappeared. After an awkwardly long silence Lauren finally spoke.

"Hi, AJ."

He tried to respond, but the flood of memories choked his brain and he was unable to deliver any words to his mouth. His lips parted slightly as he tried to speak but nothing would come out. He took a deep breath, his first since seeing her, and managed to utter her name.

"Lauren," he whispered as the torrent of images and thoughts overwhelmed his thoughts. A little smile returned to her lips.

"AJ, it's so great to see you too. There's so much that's happened since we last talked."

"Yeah, a lot has happened," he said stupidly.

After a few more seconds of awkward silence she finally asked if she could come inside and he apologized and then escorted her to the couch in the living room.

"This place is really great. I heard that you restored it yourself," she said.

"Yeah, I've spent a lot of time fixing the place up. I really like it here." There was another long silence before Connelly continued.

"So, I heard that you got that position in Berlin you really wanted."

"Yeah, it was a great post. I got to do some really amazing intel work and look over reconnaissance data that's historical legend in the field. I met a lot of people that knew my Dad and I even got to work on some projects he had started a long time ago," she explained. For the next ten minutes she described various projects she worked on while assigned to the NSA office in Berlin.

"That's fascinating. So what are you doing now that brought you to Stovall?" Connelly asked.

Lauren didn't answer; instead, her lips pursed and she fidgeted with her finger nails. She looked down at her shoes and started breathing more quickly. She finally got up off the couch quickly.

"Listen, AJ, I've got to go. There's a meeting I have to go to," she fibbed as she nervously made for the door. Connelly hopped up off the couch and caught up to her, grabbing her wrist gently. She snapped her head around and bore her gaze into Connelly's eyes. Energy, passion, fear, love, and a dozen other emotions leapt from her expression and jolted Connelly. She took her free hand and wrapped it around the back of Connelly's head as she pressed her cheek against his. He could feel a maelstrom of emotions trying to burst forth from her but she kept them capped. She kissed his cheek hard and then broke away from him and made quickly for the door. Her heels were clacking loudly on the floor and he could still hear them as she darted for the Taurus. It took only a second for her to get in the car, start the engine, and back down the driveway. In a flash she was gone down the road, just as mysteriously as she had arrived.

CHAPTER 36

One-hundred-twenty kilometers southwest of Baikonaur, near the Aral Sea in Kazakhstan, two technicians were tightening the ratchet straps securing a large container on a rail car.

"So, where is this thing getting shipped to?" one of them asked the other.

"I heard that the Iranians decided to buy it. They paid for the rest of the cost and want it shipped down there somewhere. It'll probably wind up on the black market somewhere," the other responded as he secured the strap's buckle.

"Black market! Geez, a weapon like this going to the highest bidder. Oh well," he lamented.

They finished securing the container, which was thirty-five feet long, twenty feet tall, and the width of a train car. There were only four cars in the train: a locomotive, followed by a passenger car to which the container car was attached, and a flat bed car at the end. The passenger car was occupied by five Kazak soldiers bearing Kalashnikov model 47s. The flat bed sported a 20mm chain gun, covered by a tarp, and two men huddled in a small protective hut next to it.

With little fanfare, the train left the depot in Baikonaur and headed for the Uzbekistan border. It was late that night when they crossed into Turkmenistan where they stopped briefly to refuel the train and pick up some provisions for the crew. While the train was stopped the soldiers from the passenger car casually patrolled the area in the immediate vicinity of the train. The men on the last car pulled the tarp off of the chain gun and energized its firing mechanism, then sat casually on the car floor. None of this activity alarmed anyone at the depot but no one approached the train either.

After about thirty minutes, the train pulled out of the depot and continued on its way into Iran. There was a stop just on the Iranian side of the border at which the conductor provided the border agent with a neat satchel full of official documents. Clearly recognizing the authority granted to this train crew, the agent quickly approved their entry and the train resumed its journey. It ran all day and night, making its way south through the mountains and deserts of Iran's heartland on its way to the port city of Bandar 'Abbas.

A bustling port city, Bandar 'Abbas was alive with commercial activity, most of it related to crude oil products. Tankers lined the docks with cranes and pumps running constantly. The container from the train was directed to slip 143, on the far end of the harbor. The container was lifted from the rail car by a 100-ton gantry crane and placed next to the empty slip. The five soldiers departed the passenger car and were joined by a man who emerged from the locomotive. This agent, Khomeini, was tall and muscular with a thick but well-managed bush of jet black hair on his head and a mustache to match. The agent and the five soldiers stuck close to the container car and, once it had been set down on the dock, the soldiers sat on the ground and leaned against the car. Khomeini pulled a newspaper from his pocket, spread a few pages on the ground, and sat down a few feet away from the soldiers' enclave.

Two and a half hours later, Major Gwon heard the radio crackle in the wheel house of his command ship, a freighter that they had hijacked. With a new coat of paint and forged documents, the *Chonjaeng Ponch'ang* had been sailing the seas for months without interference. Gwon now had two Zodiacs from which he conducted ever-refined pirate attacks on shipping vessels in the Atlantic and Indian Oceans as well as several other locations ripe for the picking. He had even used the *Chonjaeng Ponch'ang* three times to conduct nonviolent sales of cargo that he had stolen from other ships. It had been quite lucrative and allowed him and his band of pirates to acquire enough money for the weapon purchase a year ahead of schedule. He was confident and most pleased with his progress towards redemption.

"*Komjongsaek Pongae*, this is Safeguard," said the voice on the radio.

"This is *Komjongsaek Pongae*," he tersely replied.

"Please call our supervisor on channel 143."

"Understood," Gwon replied, understanding the coded message regarding which slip he needed to enter.

He had the helmsman proceed towards Bandar 'Abbas, about ten miles ahead, and take the ship to slip 143.

Once the *Chonjaeng Ponch'ang* was secured in the slip, Gwon walked proudly down the gangway. Khomeini stood up, brushed off his suit, and walked towards the end of the gangway where he met Gwon.

"Your package is here," Khomeini bluntly stated.

"Let me see it," Gwon said.

The two of them walked over to the container which was surrounded by five now very alert guards. Khomeini motioned that everything was all right and he escorted Gwon to a small hinged plate on one of the container's walls. He rotated the plate out of the way and handed Gwon a flashlight. It was difficult to see much through the small window but it looked very much like the photographs he had seen. It was clearly a very impressive device, the ubiquitous stainless steel smartly reflecting the flashlight beam all around the interior of the container.

Having no reason to doubt the authenticity of the weapon, he nodded and backed away from the container. He looked back to his ship and made a gesture. A minute later one of his pirates emerged from the ship with a steamer truck lashed to a hand truck. He rolled the conspicuous container down the gangway with an escort on either side. The three of them set it down on the ground next to the much, much larger container. Gwon released several locks on the trunk and opened the lid so Khomeini could inspect the contents. The tall man had to bend his creaking knees so that he could run his hands over the stacks of paper money from several countries, mostly American dollars. He spent ten minutes counting the stacks and was satisfied that the previously agreed upon bargain price of five million dollars was present.

Khomeini turned his back and gestured for two of the soldiers to take the trunk. They picked it up and the whole lot of them were gone and out of sight in less than a minute.

It took Gwon an hour to find a dock worker who could operate the gantry crane and place the container aboard the *Chonjaeng Ponch'ang*. After paying him, the pirate band spent the rest of the day securing the container to the ship's deck. They knew from their years in the Atlantic that terrific storms can come up suddenly and, although the *Chonjaeng Ponch'ang* had proven itself a very seaworthy ship, it would be easy to lose a container that was not well-secured to the deck. When they were finished and satisfied they left slip 143 and quietly made their way into the Gulf of Oman.

CHAPTER 37

Connelly was in the observation dome the next morning after Lauren left. He had a piece of sandstone that he was working with a rattail file. He made a harsh gouge in it and broke a small section off. He berated himself and tossed the file to the ground. He took a deep breath and set the broken stone on one of the cabinets. He put his head down into his hands and rubbed his eyes and forehead. He stood up, looked out over the beautiful North Carolina woods, took another deep breath and headed downstairs.

He swung open the door to his closet and pulled out a small duffel bag. He threw a few days' worth of clothes in it and a few essentials and headed for the Range Rover. The engine roared to life and he sped down the driveway of Station 65, then turning onto the road, headed north. He traced out a path on the map in his lap heading to Fort Meade in Washington D.C.

He drove quickly and arrived in metro D.C. in the early afternoon. He pulled onto the road leading to the main building of the NSA. About twenty yards short of the massive entry gate which was surrounded by concrete barriers, razor wire, and an 'observation' tower, was a small parking lot. Connelly parked the Range Rover and walked to the guard station, entering through the door. He was greeted by two security guards who were backed up by two Army Rangers with M-16 assault rifles slung over their shoulders.

"Good afternoon, Sir, how may we help you?" asked one of the guards.

"Please ring the office of Lauren Carano. My name is A.J. Connelly and I do not have an appointment," Connelly responded soberly.

The guard thumbed through a well-worn printed directory of NSA personnel which was chained to his desk. He found the number and dialed an in-house phone. After a few moments he spoke.

"Ma'am, this is Officer Drury at Gate Six. There is an 'A.J. Connelly' here to see you," the guard said.

On the other end of the line Lauren sat in her office chair stunned. It took her a moment to digest what the guard had said and reply.

"Please tell him to wait there. I'll be down in fifteen minutes," she said and then hung up the phone.

She quickly closed her computer files and logged off. She stuffed a couple of folders into her office safe, slammed it shut, and spun the dials. She threw on her coat and was down the hallway within five minutes of getting that most unexpected call. Her heart began to race as she fully realized that Connelly was here, in D.C. She was excited to see him but anxious about exactly why he was here and the fact that he was at the doorstep of the NSA.

It had only taken twelve minutes for her to arrive at Gate Six and the tires on her Taurus screeched to a halt as she parked next to Connelly's Range Rover.

"A.J., are you OK?" she asked, the concern evident on her face.

"Yeah, I'm OK but we've got to talk," he answered.

"OK, but this is a really crappy place. Follow me," she said.

She clasped his hand for a moment, staring into his eyes, and then got into her car. He followed her through the busy and winding streets of the D.C. area and finally onto a smaller residential road. She found a small parking lot that had two adjacent spaces and pulled in. Connelly looked around at his surroundings and saw that they were next to a park which had a small pond. He followed Lauren as they walked together slowly into the park.

"Lauren, I'm not entirely sure what happened in Stovall, but I was really happy to see you," Connelly led off.

There was a long silence as Lauren measured her response.

"I'm sorry about that. I had just found out that you were alive and where you had moved to. I really wanted to see you. I wasn't sure if you'd want to see me. Why didn't you call me when you got back?" she asked.

Connelly took a deep breath and exhaled.

"Well, we hadn't spoken for years, so it seemed kind of odd. After you didn't respond to my last letter I figured you didn't want to keep up a relationship," he said.

"A lot was going on then. Let's see, at that point I was assigned to a post in northern Italy. The job was pretty easy-Italy doesn't present much threat— or activity. I was also seeing someone there... but it wasn't a big deal," she said.

"Yeah, I was aboard the Eisenhower then, headed for the Pacific. I guess it would have been tough to keep up... and no real good reason to..." his voice trailed off.

After thirty seconds of silence, Lauren continued.

"There might have been a good reason. It's hard to say; like I said, a lot was going on and things were different. We were launching into our careers. It makes it tough for any relationship," she said.

They came across a bench at the edge of the pond and sat down.

"I never stopped thinking about you, Lauren. Even when I dated people I never forgot you. I mean, I dedicated myself to those relationships but there was always something missing. The excitement I always felt when I was with you didn't exist in those other relationships. There's a magic or a chemistry that I couldn't find again," he said.

Lauren smiled and her shoulders relaxed.

"I know what you mean. In Italy I dated two guys, not at the same time, of course! The first one, Francesco, was a very good-looking guy and we did some fun stuff. But, as the more my Italian and his English improved the less and less we had to say. Then there was David, built like the statue, but intellect to match. Neither one got very serious or went very far," she said.

"So, who's the lucky guy now?" Connelly asked with some trepidation.

Lauren smiled again and looked him square in the face.

"There's nobody right now," she whispered in a sultry voice.

Connelly's heart began to race as he felt surges of excitement and fear. He leaned over to her, slid his fingers around her neck, coursing through her hair. When he kissed her, a surge of energy rushed through him as though her lips were electric. His passion for her built.

When he slid closer to her on the bench she put her hand firmly on his chest and pushed him back a few inches. His eyes pressed an inquiry to her.

"Let's go to my apartment," she breathed in that sultry voice.

"I can't wait that long," Connelly pleaded.

"It's right there," she said as she pointed to a building right next to the park.

"Very nice," Connelly said, in appreciation of her foresight. They wrapped their arms around each other as they walked briskly to her apartment.

CHAPTER 38

Gwon peered through his Nikon 10x42 Monarch binoculars at the vessel approaching from the North. He had one of his bandits manning the twin coax 12.5mm gun, another with a LAW rocket against his shoulder, and a third with a Remington M24 sniper rifle crouched high in the superstructure. They watched scrupulously as the vessel approached, pulled alongside, and ultimately tethering itself to Gwon's vessel.

"Major Gwon, I presume," a tall man in navy blue fatigues shouted from his deck.

"Major Yakovlev?" Gwon answered.

"Yes. Permission to come aboard?" asked Yakovlev.

Gwon waved him over and shortly afterwards three of the Russian's crewman joined him, carrying satchels and other gear bags. Gwon had one of his men search the bags and, satisfied that they had no weapons, allowed them to disassemble the shipping crate that had been brought onboard in Bandar 'Abbas.

It took several hours for the technicians to lower the panels of the container crate but, once they had, they exposed a very, very impressive machine. It consisted of three parts, the first one a rectangular control unit eight feet long and four feet high. It had two seats molded into it for operators to sit at while working the myriad assortment of switches and readouts. The second part was a small gas-turbine generator whose inlet was about three feet in diameter and its jet-engine like fan blades a dull steel color which rattled in the breeze. The generator's electrical power went through an enormous conduit to the control unit which then delivered to the third and most important part of the contraption: the gun. Its barrel was the full length of the container and its bore was six inches. There were annuli wrapped around the barrel every half-meter, each with an inverter attached to it that led back ultimately to the control unit. The breech end was fairly simple, being little more than an access door that allowed for insertion of the projectile. A highly polished pair of servo motors were connected to a series of gears and encoders that allowed the control unit to adjust the gun's azimuth and elevation angles. A small container next to the control unit stored a half-dozen launch cartridges which allowed a projectile of almost any description to be fired from the gun. The sight of the launch cartridges brought a broad smile to Gwon's face. He was getting close to avenging the untimely loss of the ICBM and fulfilling the destiny of his country.

It took six more hours for the technicians to complete the checklist and pronounce the rail gun ready for operation. Yakovlev clapped his hands together triumphantly.

"Major, it is time to start the gun!" he said with glee as he motioned to have the generator turbine started.

A series of clicks followed by the low-pitch whine of the starter motor filled the previously quiet air around the ships. Twenty seconds later, the sound increased significantly as the fuel flow to the burner began, resulting in a blue flame appearing in the exhaust port. Once the readings on the engine stabilized, Yakovlev donned a pair of ear muffs and offered a pair to Gwon who dismissed them with a wave of his hand. Yakovlev smiled and then gestured for the engine to be run up to full speed. A minute later the engine roared at full speed and the sound had escalated to a deafening roar. Gwon reluctantly took the ear muffs as his crewmembers scrambled through their gear for ear plugs like the ones Yakovlev's men had put in an hour ago.

The control unit came to life as one of Gwon's men, Ahn, studied the actions of the technician operating the machine. He had been studying the manual for hours but needed to watch closely since he would be operating the machine eventually. When the control unit's internal checks completed, the operator manually slewed the gun barrel left to right then up and down. He then reached over and flipped a switch which engaged the auto-track function. This function would continually adjust the gun barrel's azimuth and elevation to keep it locked on a predetermined target point.

The technician asked Yakovlev for a target point and, although the gun could fire up to 250 miles, he selected one only one mile away so that they could view the impact. Yakovlev removed a dummy round from the storage bin and showed Gwon how to insert it into the breech of the rail gun. They both then stepped back to the control unit and signaled the operator to fire the gun.

After pressing the big red button, the operator did nothing but watch the display as the turbine generator fed an enormous amount of electrical power to the control unit which eventually turned it into a staggeringly powerful magnetic field that grabbed the highly ferrous launch cartridge and yanked it forward from the breech. When the cartridge reached the first annulus the control unit switched the magnetic field to the next annulus to further accelerate the cartridge and propel it towards the muzzle end of the barrel.

By the time the cartridge reached the muzzle it was traveling several times the speed of sound and made a thundering 'wump' sound as it left the barrel. Almost instantaneously the projectile covered the mile-long trip to the target and crashed into the water's surface with colossal energy. The water burst into a wall of frothy white chaos which reached upward nearly 100 feet and took almost a minute to dissipate. Gwon was so excited by the destructive potential of this weapon that he couldn't suppress the big toothy smile that monopolized his face.

The gun was shut down and the mighty turbine generator turned off, to the relief of everyone from both ships. Several more hours were spent with Yakovlev's crew training Gwon's men on the gun's operation. Eventually both sides felt confident in the transition of knowledge and Yakovlev's men left for their ship. Both sides manned their weapons in case the deal went sour at the last moment, but the satchel Gwon gave Yakovlev, containing $100,000 in U.S. paper currency, was satisfactory and the ships parted ways without violence.

Gwon returned to the charthouse and plotted their next course.

CHAPTER 39

In the morning, Connelly got out of bed, put on a robe, and quietly made his way into Lauren's kitchen. After a minute of searching he had found some eggs, bacon, and rolls and started the coffee maker. The crackling sound of the bacon roused Lauren and she slipped a silk robe around her naked body and made her way into the kitchen.

"So, you know how to do *two* things really well, I see," she said friskily.

"Yeah, but that's it. Beyond these two things, I'm useless," he replied with a relaxed smile.

When he finished making breakfast, they took their plates to the small but pleasant balcony which overlooked the park where they talked the previous evening. Lauren noticed Connelly looking at the sun which had just risen over the eastern horizon.

"Do you like watching the sunrise?" she asked.

"Yeah. Yeah, it's something I started doing a couple of years ago," he replied, pensively. Lauren watched him closely as she sipped her coffee.

"On March 29th, 2007, I hopped in a U-2 on the deck of the *U.S.S. Nimitz.* A couple of hours later, I was shot down by a ballistic missile. The North Koreans didn't take too well to my uninvited visit and booked me into a room at the 'Pyongyang Hilton'. There weren't many things to look forward to each day, but I made a deal with the sunrise that if it would come up then I would watch it. Even on overcast mornings I could tell that it was holding up its end of the bargain so I held up mine. I still watch the sunrise, even in Stovall," he said.

Lauren stayed very quiet, the only sound coming from her slippers anxiously scraping on the ground. Connelly spent the next hour describing his experience in the POW camp, including the friendship he cultivated with Shin. He told her about his enduring interest in stone carving but never mentioned the jade figurine he had carved of her.

By the time he had finished the description of his horrific stay in Korea, Lauren had slid into his arms, partly to stay warm in the cool morning air but also because she wanted to touch him. They spent an hour more on the balcony until they were both chilled and went inside. Back in the kitchen, Connelly was rinsing off the plates when Lauren came up behind him and wrapped her arms around his chest. She caressed his chest and slipped her hands underneath his robe, running her fingers through the hair on his chest. She gently pulled the robe off of his shoulders with a naughty look in her eye but then took a step back with a horrified look on her face. After a few seconds, Connelly turned to see her look. He picked the robe up off the floor and put it back on.

"I guess you didn't see that last night," Connelly offered softly.

It took Lauren a few seconds to close her mouth and collect her senses.

"No, it was dark..." she mumbled.

The mishmash of scars on his back were like some ghastly Jackson Pollock painting. She had to sit down on one of the bar stools and Connelly sat next to her. He spent a few minutes describing the various ways he accumulated the scars but never gave all of the gory details. She sat stunned for several minutes.

"I can't believe Gwon did that to you. It wasn't in the files..." she said softly.

It took a few seconds for Connelly to absorb what she had said. With each passing second his pulse quickened and his face turned a darker shade of red.

"What did you say?" he asked in an irritated voice.

Lauren snapped out of her daze as her pulse quickened too.

"Oh, nothing," she replied.

Connelly stood up and squared his shoulders to her.

"I never told you his name!" Connelly declared. He continued, "You knew about this? What do you mean 'files'?" he charged excitedly.

Lauren quickly got off the stool and moved towards Connelly as he backed off. Her fingers and toes got cold as the adrenaline started to surge in her veins. Connelly made his way for the bedroom where he rapidly got dressed.

"A.J., no! I didn't... I mean, I wasn't—" Lauren tried desperately.

"I can't believe you've known all along! And you didn't tell me that you knew! Jesus Christ- why did you really come to Stovall? What files are you talking about? Is there a current mission underway? What the hell, Lauren?" he shouted as he made the way to the door with Lauren clinging hopelessly behind him.

"No, A.J., don't leave!" she pleaded. "I can explain!" she cried as he flung the door open and charged down the hall.

Lauren collapsed in the doorway of her apartment, tears running down her face. She clasped her hands over her face.

"Oh, A.J.!" she softly moaned as he descended the stairwell in a flurry of footsteps and swears.

CHAPTER 40

Rhee sat stiffly in the break room at the fuel processing station in King's Bay Naval Submarine Base on the coast on Georgia, sharing a table with two other blue-collar workers of indisputable American heritage.

"Shit, Joey, there ain't no fuckin' way the Packers are gonna win the division this year! Their new starting quarterback is already in jail and half the defensive line failed drug tests! No way, man. This is the year for the Chargers!" declared Frank.

"The Chargers?! They couldn't win a game of tic-tac-toe even if you spotted 'em two X's!" Joey replied.

"You're crazy... I bet Rhee here can give us this year's winner. So, Rhee, who do you bet on for this year?" Frank asked.

Rhee, whose blue jumpsuit was impeccably clean as was his white hardhat, blinked a couple of times and then looked at Frank.

"I do not care for your American football. Therefore, I do not have any predictions for the outcome of the sporting season," he replied evenly.

"Shit, Rhee, you've been here for nine years- how can you not follow the NFL?" he asked incredulously but got no answer.

Upstairs, in an office overlooking the main loading floor of the naval base, Myeong studied his computer screen carefully. He clicked the mouse on the file name 'TA-KBNB' which brought up a calendar showing the Travel Authorization for King's Bay Naval Base. He quickly went to the current day and confirmed that Captain Hartley, the base's commanding officer, was on travel in Washington, D.C. He then pulled a file showing the scheduled deliveries and outgoing shipments for that day. He found the entry marked 'SNF- shipment 621-G' and opened the entry. The records for Spent Nuclear Fuel were always lengthy and complicated, worthy of the cargo they represented which was nuclear fuel that had been removed from a nuclear-powered submarine. After fourteen years the radioactive material would decay to the point where it was not powerful enough to drive a submarine or an aircraft carrier anymore but it was still highly toxic and had to be handled carefully. The documentation and ledger entries were lengthy and numerous but the automatic Unix computer script that Myeong had written and just run on the computer updated everything associated with shipment 621-G, reclassifying its contents as 'M-NT', metallic nontoxic. With these markings and classification, the crate containing several pounds of nuclear fuel would be handled by everyone in the system as though it were a box full of worn out bearings and chipped gears. Myeong typed in a final set of commands and then walked over to the window.

Rhee could see Myeong nod through the window and immediately walked over to the computer printer at a work station in the shipping bay. He pulled the three fresh pages off the printer and discreetly replaced three other pages in the shipping manifest log with the counterfeit ones. As he replaced the clipboard on the hook on the wall he grabbed a meter out of his toolbox and slipped it into his pocket.

Forty-five minutes later, a 2-ton truck backed into loading dock and the two armed soldiers in the back lowered the tailgate. Inside the warehouse Joey had just started up a forklift and drove it over to the part of the warehouse where Frank and Rhee were waiting next to shipment 621-G. Frank, being the senior loading technician, picked up the manifest clipboard and flipped to the record for 621-G. His eyebrows furled tightly.

"This manifest says 621-G is nontoxic metallics! Why the hell is it packed in a spent nuke case?" he asked angrily.

"I don't know. Let me check with the geiger counter," Rhee replied.

Rhee pulled the meter out of his pocket and inserted the probe into the access port on the crate. Frank examined the readings on the gauge, which were hovering around one point two.

"That's nothing but normal background radiation. There ain't no spent nukes in this box. Damn lazy bastards used a two million dollar nuke case to ship garbage out of here! Shit, people wonder where the waste, fraud, and abuse are! It's right here..."

He continued to mumble curses as he waved Joey over with the forklift. Rhee slipped his modified meter back into his pocket and helped secure the crate onto the forks and escorted it out to the loading dock. The soldiers in the back of the 2-ton stood up when they saw the crate but Frank waved them off and directed the forklift to a conventional flatbed truck.

"What's going on? I thought we had an SNF shipment to go out tonight," the 2-ton truck drive asked.

"Yeah, it's a fuck-up in the warehouse. They used a nuke box to put regular garbage in. I'm not gonna waste you guys on that garbage- I'll get a regular driver to take this shit to the dump. Sorry for the mixup- have a great night!" Frank said.

A few eyebrows were raised as the SNF container underwent inspection at the gate but the guards were satisfied with the signatures and allowed the truck to leave with its driver being the only occupant.

As the truck rounded a corner three miles from the base, three men clad in black outfits were waiting, crouched low in the scrub brush. When the truck ran over the five-hundred caltrops scattered on the road, all six of its tires exploded. The truck was only going thirty-five miles per hour and as such the driver was able to bring it to a controlled stop fairly quickly. He hopped out of the truck, let out a deep exhale, and walked to the truck's rear axle where he examined the pair of shredded tires. He ran his hand over the tread of the outer tire and cut his finger on the needle-sharp point of the caltrop stuck in the tire. He carefully pulled it out and held it up in the moonlight to examine it. Just as he got a good view of it, a 7.62mm rifle round ripped through his chest. A moment later he collapsed on the ground and the caltrop fell harmlessly out of his grip.

The three pirates moved on the crate and, using an oxyacetylene torch, had the SNF create opened in under three minutes. Using the stolen diagrams and instruction provided by Myeong and Rhee, they were able to extract the inner container with the spent nuclear fuel and load it onto a specially-outfitted Zodiac in under twenty minutes. Gwon took the helm and raced out to sea where the *Chonjaeng Ponch'ang* awaited him.

CHAPTER 41

Dixie brought his Camaro to a gentle stop about ten feet behind Connelly's Range Rover which was haphazardly parked diagonally across the driveway of Station 65. He saw that the Rover had, in fact, knocked a softball-sized chunk of cement out of the station's front edifice when its bumper made contact. Dixie walked slowly towards the front door of the station, alerted by the fact that the front door was open about a foot. He pushed the door open and took a couple of cautious steps inside and looked around. He was startled to see the main living room looking like a bomb had gone off in it. All of the chairs were knocked over and two of them had more than one broken leg; the coffee table was turned over, the vase that used to be on it now smashed against a wall; the napkin holder, sweeteners, and cup rack had been summarily swiped off the counter and the painting on the far wall was severely tilted. The only piece of furniture that looked undamaged was the sofa and that presently had a severely disheveled A.J. Connelly on top of it.

Dixie found the coffee pot which, miraculously, was undamaged and he brewed a pot of strong Kona without waking Connelly. He set a large, full cup on the ground under Connelly's head so that the aromatic vapors could not fail to get into his nose. After five minutes Connelly finally came to life with a snort and a start. He raised his hand to rub his face.

"Hey, Dixie," Connelly said.

Dixie lifted his cup of coffee to his mouth as he spoke.

"Girl trouble?" Dixie asked.

Connelly stretched for a moment and managed to straighten himself up on the sofa. He looked around at the damage he had done to the room.

"Ah, shit. Yeah, kind of," he replied.

Connelly sipped the coffee as he slumped back onto the sofa. After a minute of collecting himself he began to tell Dixie about his visit with Lauren.

"Sounds to me like some serious shit is going on... but it also sounds like you blew up a little quick," Dixie said.

"Yeah, I know," he replied, shaking his head as he closed his eyes. He continued, "I really didn't realize how close the Korea shit is to the surface. As soon as she hinted that she knew about what I went through and that she knows something about Gwon, I lost it. There was a lot of fury boiling down inside me and, I guess, it came out."

Dixie sat quietly as he listened to Connelly tell his story.

"You know, Gwon beat me up just about every day. The only times he didn't was when he was too drunk to connect with my jaw. On those days he would spit on me or just poke around with his combat knife. I hate that bastard," Connelly said.

"Sounds like a bad guy," Dixie said.

"Bad like an epidemic virus. It took me a long time to learn how to bury the memories of him. I thought I had gotten rid of them."

Dixie stood up and looked earnestly at Connelly.

"A.J., you needed this," he said as he gestured around the room. He continued, "What happened to you in Korea was very, very intense and it will always be with you. It's not a matter of forgetting it or burying it. It will always be there and it will always affect you. The best thing you can do for yourself is work your way through the emotions."

"Work through them? It doesn't look so helpful," Connelly said, referring to the piles of destroyed furniture.

"This is a mourning process. It's not easy," Dixie said.

"Mourning? Mourning whom?" Connelly asked.

"You're going to have to mourn the years you lost over there. You'll also have to mourn the loss of the view of the world you had before that happened. That may sound all new-age, hoodoo-voodoo, but the essence of it is real. You've lost something and you have to mourn it."

"OK, so how do I do that without destroying what little I've managed to build for myself since then?" Connelly asked.

"That's a journey that's yours and yours all alone. The only thing I know about mourning is that you've got to do it on its own schedule. Don't force yourself to mourn it according to some schedule. When it comes, accept it and work through it; if it's not there, don't go looking for it. It's like the sunrise- it'll come on its own damn schedule. Just make sure the blinds are open."

Connelly nodded and looked back into his coffee cup as he contemplated his friend's advice.

"This afternoon I'll bring the pickup over and we load the trash up into it. Maybe tomorrow we can go into Raleigh and get you some new furniture," Dixie said.

Connelly thanked him and saw him to the door. He finished his cup of coffee and then began sorting through the debris.

CHAPTER 42

Aboard the *Chonjaeng Ponch'ang*, Gwon looked over the shoulder of Ahn, his chief technician. He had selected the members of his pirate band very carefully, making sure that he had garnered a sufficient collection of secondary talents to cover the various tasks that would be required of the team in their mission. Ahn was seated at a workbench in a shop on one of the lower decks of the ship. He had two work areas segregated, each with an almost identical collection of parts, including a launch cartridge for the rail gun. The seat at which he was currently working had a small explosive charge that he was wiring to a circuit board designed to fit inside the launch cartridge. He also had a ten-pound white phosphor slug in the shape of a squat cylinder. He carefully assembled the parts as Gwon's breath puffed onto his shoulder.

CHAPTER 43

Two weeks later, Connelly had replaced or fixed all of the furniture in his living room and was spending the afternoon at the airport helping Dixie work on the turbine engines of the Twin Otter. After they completed a routine inspection of the engine they retired to Dixie's domicile, a modest structure attached to the main hangar. Since the work was completed, they popped open a couple of beers and sat on the sofa, talking as the TV prattled on in the background.

In the middle of one of Dixie's sentences, Connelly's attention was diverted by a report on CNN. Connelly hadn't been looking at the screen and the volume was low, but some unmistakable sounds had pierced his memory. He couldn't place it at first. Dixie slowed down as he could see Connelly's brow furled tightly.

"What is it?" Dixie asked.

"I...I can't be sure," he mumbled as he walked over to the television and turned the volume up.

"To follow up on our report from last week, we have managed to obtain an interview with the truck driver, taped at his hospital bed shortly before he died."

The screen cut from the anchor to a tape of a man in a hospital bed, struggling to say something into the camera. The various tubes and wires had been pulled aside, allowing him to talk.

"He said,'chon yang pon chang', or something like that. He wasn't speaking English. It was Japanese or something. I can't remember much else..." the dying man said.

Connelly was glued to the screen and his blood ran cold when he heard what the man had said. Even though the man's memory was poor and his southern accent twisted the words considerably, Connelly had no doubts that he had said, 'war and prosperity' in Korean. His heart was pounding in his chest as he realized that Gwon was not only still alive but had just hijacked a shipment leaving a naval base only a few hundred miles away from where he lived. His stomach turned and he had to sit down.

"What the hell is it, AJ?" Dixie demanded.

"It's Gwon. He's here," Connelly said.

CHAPTER 44

Conference room YA-6 at the NSA's Fort Meade facility was buzzing with activity. Representatives from the NRO, CIA, FBI, Coast Guard, and the military branches were there. Lauren sat down next to Jurgensen as he called the meeting to order.

"Gentlemen, we've got a serious situation on our hands. As you know, two weeks ago a shipment from King's Bay was hijacked and thirty-two pounds of nuclear fuel were stolen," Jurgensen said.

"Excuse me," a Coast Guard captain interrupted, "but I haven't been brought up to speed on this. Is this weapons grade material?"

"No, this is spent fuel. It was removed from the *USS Wyoming* due to life cycle considerations. It is too weak for making a weapon, without considerable reprocessing," Jurgensen explained.

"So what's the big deal?" an FBI rep asked.

"The big deal, as you say, is that this material is highly toxic and still very radioactive. It will cause very serious health problems to anyone exposed to it," Jurgensen explained.

"It's thirty pounds, right? How big is that? The size of a bowling ball? Should be easy to find and recover before more than a dozen people get exposed to it, right?" the Coast Guard captain asked.

"It's not that simple. The potential use of this material as a weapon is quite grave. If the material were ground into a powder and spread via an airborne weapon, creating a 'powder rain', those 'measly' thirty pounds could affect an area the size of, say, Washington D.C. Everyone would be exposed; the water would be tainted, the fields contaminated, every breath of air would be toxic. Within hours, seventy-five percent of the population would be suffering from severe radiation poisoning effects. In a few weeks, half of those people would die. The duration and extent of the impact is hard to calculate with any further certainty."

Although Jurgensen gave no further details, the room had fallen silent at the prospect of Washington or New York being devastated and thrown into a state of chaos. After a minute of contemplation, questions and suggestions on how to recover the material and prepare for an attack were flying from all corners of the conference room. In the end, the Coast Guard was detailed to conduct extensive inspections of any ship approaching an east coast port. The Navy would supplement this effort and the Air Force would fly meticulous patrols to see if any ships or aircraft approached without permission. The Army and the NRO would supplement the FBI's ground efforts to search for the material and the NSA would coordinate the operation.

After the dust settled, Jurgensen asked Lauren to meet with him in his office.

"Lauren, even though the trail's cold, I'd like for you to go to King's Bay and see if you can learn anything more from the workers there; interview the guards, the trash guys, the orderlies at the hospital- everybody."

"Yes Sir," she replied.

"Get Connelly too," Jurgensen said without looking up from his desk.

Lauren did not want to explain what had happened between her and Connelly although she knew that Jurgensen's request would not be easy to fulfill.

"Yes Sir," she replied and turned for her office.

'No idea how I'm going to do that?' she thought to herself as she hurried into her office to get her things ready for the trip to Stovall and then on to Savannah.

CHAPTER 45

After a grueling week of precision machining and assembly, Ahn, who had been assembling the two launch cartridges, presented Gwon with the first one.

"Sir, it is ready to be tested," he said as he stood at attention.

Gwon took the projectile and looked it over very carefully. He then gave it back to Ahn and walked quickly to the bridge.

"Change course, heading zero-three-five, three-quarters ahead," Gwon barked.

The helmsman acknowledged the order and whipped the wheel to the right to come on course as the engines throttled up and pushed the ship ahead. Gwon then had Ahn install the projectile into the breech of the rail gun and perform the various pre-firing checks that were needed.

Three hours later, Gwon ordered the helm to stop the *Chonjaeng Ponch'ang* about three miles southwest of a small island that was roughly round and about six miles in diameter. Gwon took out his Nikon 8x50 binoculars and studied the island. After a thorough examination, he ordered the ship to circle the island as he examined it through the lenses. Having satisfied himself that the island was deserted, he turned his attention to the radar screen and made sure that no air or sea vessels were anywhere nearby. He then ordered the *Chonjaeng Ponch'ang* back to the original position three miles southwest of the small island.

"Ahn, here are the coordinates. Bring the gun online and program it for this target," Gwon ordered.

Ahn immediately engaged the turbine power generator that would give the rail gun its needed massive electrical supply.

With ear muffs securely in place, he turned to the gun and flipped the switches that brought the control console to life. He worked as quickly as he could, without being reckless, and finally entered the coordinates Gwon had given him, targeting the center of the small island they had observed.

"Sir, the coordinates have been entered and the weapon is ready," Ahn stated.

Gwon took a last look at the island which was fading into the darkness of the fast approaching dusk.

"Fire!" Gwon shouted over the roar of the generator.

Ahn turned back to the console, checked several instrument readouts, and then activated the firing sequence. As it had before, the massive gun emitted a whine as its electric coils became energized and then, suddenly, with a tremendous 'whump' sound, hurled the projectile from its muzzle and sent it racing through the air. Moments later the dimming sky was set ablaze as the warhead exploded, dispersing the phosphor charge which burned a bright white. Often white phosphor is used to create a flare by setting a ball of it on fire, but in this case the explosive charge turned the phosphor powder into a burning umbrella that spread out like the wings of a bird of prey descending on the island.

"Helm, all ahead, flank speed!" Gwon shouted.

Seconds later the ship surged ahead and raced towards the burning island. Ahn, sitting at the control console, looked back at Gwon and could see the bright light of the burning island reflected in the teeth showing through Gwon's wicked smile.

The ship made another circular pass around the island as Gwon studied the burning foliage on the island. By the time the ship had finished its circuit, Gwon was skipping across the deck with delight at the fact that the explosive charge in the projectile had managed to propel small chunks of the phosphor to every reach of the island, essentially blanketing an area six miles in diameter with the fiery material. Satisfied that the design and function of the explosive projectile was satisfactory, Gwon turned his back to the conflagration and ordered the ship on its next course.

CHAPTER 46

The light on Jurgensen's phone started blinking. He glanced at it and noticed that it was line four. His pulse quickened. Line four was reserved for urgent business that was of national security implications only. He snatched the receiver.

"Jurgensen," he said.

"Sir, this is Mackovitz, we have some data you should see," said the voice.

"I'll be right there," he replied.

Jurgensen closed the folder on his desk and immediately made for the basement of the building where the urgent intelligence messages arrived. After passing through the numerous and elaborate security checkpoints, he arrived in the data center where Mackovitz waved him over to a computer screen that four people were looking at intently.

"What do yo have?" Jurgensen asked.

"Twenty-two minutes ago an Air Force ICBM early-warning satellite lit up like the fourth of July," Mackovitz said.

"Holy shit- the Russians have launched a nuke?!" Jurgensen shouted incredulously.

Mackovitz gestured to him that that was not the case.

"No, no, it's not a launch. It's something weird, though. This location is in the Atlantic, about two hundred miles east of Bermuda. Obviously, nobody has an ICBM launch site there and the satellite data ruled out a ballistic submarine launch," he explained.

"Then what the hell is it?" Jurgensen asked.

Mackovitz shrugged his shoulders. "We don't know yet. It looks like an area, a large area, suddenly burst into flames. The satellite detected a tremendous, sudden surge in infrared radiation that accompanies a large missile launch. A building or forest fire doesn't set it off because those start slowly and grow over a period of minutes or hours. This thing went from ice cold to burning hot-shit in a second. The whole damn area, which is a bit more than twenty-five square miles, is burning. We don't know what the fuck happened."

"Call the Navy and have them get some assets over there ASAP to find out what the hell is going on," Jurgensen said as he studied the colorful display on the computer screen showing the burning area in an otherwise 'cold' ocean.

CHAPTER 47

Lauren arrived in Stovall at seven-fifteen p.m. and pulled into the driveway at Station 65. She walked up to the front door slowly, noticing that none of the lights were on inside. She knocked on the door a couple of times and waited a few minutes and then went back to her car.

A few minutes later, she pulled into the parking lot at Benson's which had its usual half-dozen patrons that seemed to be part of the décor. She took a seat at the bar and asked for a cup of coffee. Suzy lazily slid a tepid cup of coffee to her and turned her back on Lauren to wash some dishes.

"Excuse me," Lauren said softly. After a few seconds she repeated herself more loudly and Suzy turned around with a surly expression on her face.

"I'm looking for AJ Connelly," she explained.

Suzy replied with a blank stare.

"Do you know where he is?" Lauren asked, a bit piqued.

"Nope," was the monosyllabic response from Suzy.

Realizing she was going to get nowhere with this waitress, she turned and scanned the other patrons of the diner who minded their own business. With no help to be found at Benson's, Lauren left and drove back to Station 65, parking in the driveway and reclining the seat to be more comfortable.

Three hours later, she was alerted by the dim rays of light that had come on inside the station. She slipped her shoes back on, got out of the car, and approached the front door of the station.

Connelly took a deep breath, straightened his shirt and walked towards the door, opening it just as Lauren arrived on the stoop.

"AJ, I—," Lauren started when Connelly interrupted her.

"No, Lauren, I'm so sorry for what I said back in D.C. It's been tough and... " he stammered, his voice trailing off to nothing.

Lauren looked down for a moment then entered through the open door. She and Connelly walked into the living room and sat on the couch. As Connelly's brow furled deeply and his breathing became labored as he went over in his head what had happened at Lauren's apartment. Seeing his anguish, Lauren scooted a bit closer to him and put her warm hand gently on the side of his neck. The soft, comforting touch immediately eased the tension in Connelly's face and his breathing softened.

She looked over his body and could tell that he had spent a lot of time since his escape rebuilding his body. Starting with a very lean condition, his muscles were well-defined and attractive, his bland and sparse diet not allowing for enough fat to fill in under his jaw or in his shoulders. Even though he was wearing a collared, button-down shirt, she could see two of his myriad scars, one slicing up his left collar bone and the other descending mercilessly from his right temple. Her heart fluttered a little as the contrast of construction and destruction in his body turned her on. A tide swelled in her and carried her body closer to his, finally lifting her onto his lap, face-to-face. With her legs spread apart and her skirt bunched up to her waist, she clasped his face between her hands and kissed him softly but passionately, her lips and tongue gliding across his in a controlled frenzy.

Connelly swept his arms around her and pulled her hard against him, his fear and confusion quickly melting away and being supplanted by a rush of excitement and lust.

Suddenly, Lauren pulled her lips away and pressed Connelly's head to her shoulder, both of them panting heavily. She quickly slid off of him, her fingers gently sliding off the side of his face. She straightened her skirt and brushed the nonexistent dust off of her jacket and looking awkwardly around the room. Connelly stood up and came close to her.

"Lauren, what's wrong?" Connelly asked.

"AJ, this is all very... exciting, but there's something else we've got to talk about it. It's really why I came here, I mean, I came to see you but there's something else," she blurted.

They took a moment to calm down and relocated to the counter in the kitchen where Connelly started brewing a pot of coffee.

"Do you know Mack Jurgensen?" she asked.

"Yes, I do," Connelly replied with loathing in his voice.

"Well, he sent me to Savannah to look into the theft of some radioactive material and he wanted me to take you with me," she said.

She explained what they knew about the incident at King's Bay and why they were concerned. Connelly agreed to go with her and quickly packed a bag. They left Stovall in her Taurus that night and drove all night to arrive in Savannah the next morning.

They slept for a few hours, exhausted from the all-night drive, and arrived at the naval base shortly before lunch. They conducted interviews with everyone connected to the incident and took notes. They inspected the area where the ambush had taken place but found no new clues regarding the attack. By evening they were through and headed back to the Marriott Hotel on the riverwalk.

Once they were back in their room, Lauren let out an exhausted sigh and kicked her shoes off as she made her way over to the mirror next to the bathroom.

"I am exhausted and I am going to take a shower," she said with mock defiance as she scratched her scalp, not noticing Connelly approaching her.

She was slightly startled when his hands slipped around her sides and met in front, then started their way upwards.

"Oh my..." she said with a naughty, salacious grin overtaking her face.

Connelly's hands unbuttoned her blouse slowly, starting at the top and proceeding downward. Once her blouse was open, his hands caressed her chest as she reached back to run her hands through his hair.

"You said you wanted to take a shower," Connelly said, "but there's a jacuzzi tub over there. What do you say?"

No verbal answer was necessary and within minutes soapy water was rhythmically splashing over the edge of the jacuzzi tub.

The next morning they got up early, reluctantly, and headed back to Stovall. Over the course of the five hour drive they talked mostly about Lauren's experiences in Berlin and Rome. As they got closer to Stovall Lauren got more serious and quiet.

"Lauren, are you all right?" Connelly asked.

"Yeah, I'm just worried about... Gwon. This situation could get really dangerous," she said distractedly.

"Yeah, I guess it could... but we can't worry about it too much right now," he said, squinting his eyes slightly as he looked at her.

There was very little else said until they pulled into the driveway at Station 65. As they were pulling to a stop Connelly said, "I can't wait to show you the sunrise from the observation dome here- it's really spectacular..." His voice drifted off as he realized that Lauren did not shut off the motor and kept her seatbelt buckled as Connelly started to get out of the car.

"Lauren?" he asked.

She looked down at her hands and spoke without looking at him. "I've got to get back to Fort Meade and make my report. They're waiting for me," she answered.

Connelly waited for more of an explanation but didn't get one.

"Is everything OK, Lauren? I mean, between us?" he asked.

She looked up at him quickly and answered. "Yeah, everything's fine. Just fine," she said. "I'm just concerned and I've got to go, really. I'll call you when I get back to D.C." she said and then she leaned over and kissed him quickly.

Connelly got his bag and watched as she backed the Taurus down the driveway and sped away from him.

CHAPTER 48

Gwon could see the horizon through the pothole in his cabin bob up and down as the ship gently rolled back and forth with the ocean's waves. He had been watching the edge of the Earth for hours when his view was blocked by one of his men passing in front of the porthole. The same man knocked on the door of Gwon's cabin a moment later.

"Yes, what is it Ryu?" Gwon lazily replied.

"Sir, may I come in?" the man requested.

Ryu came into the room with a deliberate reverence in his step. He timidly sat in a chair next to Gwon, who was lying on his bunk.

"Sir, we have been drifting on the ocean for three weeks. May I humbly ask what our plans our?"

Gwon sat up in his bunk and swung his legs over the side, his eyes piercing Ryu's.

"We are going to strike at the heart of the oppressors who have unfairly kept their thumb on us. It will be a glorious day," he said.

Ryu waited for a minute and carefully chose to continue.

"Yes, Sir, this is a most worthy cause which I am looking forward to with great anticipation. Of course, my unswerving devotion to you and this cause go without saying, but my desire for action grows as my patriotism races through my blood," Ryu explained.

Gwon smiled and appreciated the delicate way that his subordinate had phrased his feelings.

"Ryu, the day will be here soon. We must get close to the coast of the United States in order to strike at them. Even with our magnificent new weapon, we must be within two-hundred kilometers of the target for an accurate shot. Right now, the

United States Navy, Air Force, and Coast Guard, along with their sinister array of orbiting satellites, are looking for us. The patrols along their coastline are thick and they are acting in their usual arrogant manner, searching every ship that comes near. We must wait until the time is right," Gwon said.

"And when will the time be right?" Ryu asked excitedly.

Gwon leaned in towards Ryu.

"The gods of war and prosperity will find a way to get us to our target. They will pave the way and give me a sign that we are to follow that path. Their mighty plow will carve a road through the infidel's pompous barrier and open the sky for us to strike. We must be patient but the gods will give us the way," Gwon said.

"Yes Sir, Captain!" Ryu excitedly replied and hopped out of the chair. He turned and left the cabin with a sprightly step.

Gwon walked over to the porthole and looked out at the edge of the sea and then up at the sky.

"Yes, you will show me the way..." he whispered to the sky.

CHAPTER 49

For a week Connelly called Lauren's number and left messages on her answering machine asking her to call him. He knew that something more than the Gwon crisis was bothering her but he felt that driving up there and surprising her again was a bad idea.

On the other end of the line, Lauren had skipped messages that had Connelly's number attached to them on the caller ID. On one occasion she happened to be home when he called and she intentionally turned the volume up on the TV to drown out the scared voice being recorded on the tape.

Finally, at twenty past midnight on a Tuesday, Lauren picked up the phone and dialed Connelly's number.

"Hello?" he answered.

"AJ, it's Lauren," she said softly.

"Lauren, are you OK? I've tried to call several times... I was worried about you," he said.

She didn't say anything for a while before answering him.

"AJ, I just can't do this. I think I really like you... I might be..." her voice was choked off in her throat.

"Lauren, I feel the same way. Since I've seen you again I've felt better than I have in a long, long time. I'm definitely healing, emotionally, I mean, and—"

She interrupted him, "That's just it, AJ. I don't think I can be there while you heal. It's something you've got to do on your own and I'm just too involved with you to be there, if that makes sense," she said.

"No, it doesn't, I don't think. Lauren, I feel great around you and I think, I hope, that you feel that way around me. I know I've got some ground to cover but I think I can offer you a lot along the way. I've felt very strongly about you for a long time- you'll never know how much I've thought about you over the years. I love you. I've loved you for a long time," he said.

Tears ran down her face and the muscles in her throat tightened around her vocal cords.

"AJ, I just can't," she said with all the strength she could muster. Then she hung up the phone and cried so hard her tears soaked the silk camisole she was wearing. She rolled over on her side and pulled the blanket up over herself and, eventually, mercifully, fell asleep under intense exhaustion.

CHAPTER 50

Onboard the Coast Guard cutter *Yosemite*, Commander Daryl Allison stood stiffly against the gunwale with his executive officer next to him.

"Dammit, Ken, how are we supposed to find this shithead? There's a thousand ships and ten million square miles of salt water out there and they want us to snag this one guy that they can't identify, describe, or recognize," the captain said.

"Don't know, Cap'n. Half of the damn Atlantic Fleet is roaming the eastern seaboard and the Air Force's recon assets are swarming the skies from Maine to Florida. God help anybody who capsizes in the Gulf of Mexico. And it's open season for terrorists to run amuck anywhere else in the world since all our eyes are here," he replied.

The captain raised his binoculars and looked out over the sea, confirming that there was nothing there that his naked eyes hadn't seen. The exec's radio crackled to life and he listened to the incoming message.

"Cap'n, the *USS Seawolf* reports that she is eight miles to our south, ready to swap search grids with us," he reported.

"Yeah, OK. Let's keep the bad guys guessing about what billion-dollar asset is churning holes in the water looking for him. Tell the *Seawolf* that we'll execute the standard departure and take over their grid," he said.

CHAPTER 51

Gwon's crew endured another two months at sea. Aside from two attacks on shipping vessels to gain supplies, they did little except for maintaining the ship and trying to entertain themselves. The crew was getting restless and Gwon was privately getting antsy, anxious for the opportunity to fulfill his destiny and strike the U.S. Then, on the fourth day of October, he saw the opportunity on the radar screen for which he had waited so long.

"Captain Gwon, there is a major storm three hundred miles southwest of our position," Ryu reported.

"Yes, I see it. It is a major hurricane... which way is it moving?" he asked.

Ryu worked his keyboard furiously, compiling data from the ship's onboard weather radar as well as the wealth of data he obtained from satellite-based internet data flows. NOAA and the NHC had been providing copious data about Hurricane *Valerie* to a number of government agencies and Ryu was able to easily intercept the data as well as utilize NOAA's own website information.

"It is moving north-northwest at twenty-five miles per hour. NOAA's six computer models for storm track forecast, which usually disagree, are quite in agreement on the path of this one," Ryu said as he brought up the web page displaying the most likely path projection of *Valerie*. "It is headed almost directly for Washington, D.C."

Gwon's smile cut across his face like a fissure left over from a magnitude seven earthquake.

"The gods are driving their plow through the barricade," Gwon whispered to himself. "And we will follow it in."

"Ryu," Gwon spoke up, "plot a course to bring us to this point," he said as he gestured to a specific location on the map. "I want us their in exactly fourteen hours. No less, no more."

Ryu acknowledged the order and computed the speed and heading, which he relayed to the helm. Finally, the diesel motors thundered to life and the *Chonjaeng Ponch'ang* was underway again to the delight of the restless pirate crew.

Precisely fourteen hours later the *Chonjaeng Ponch'ang* slowed to a stop at the predetermined location. Gwon stepped out of the bridge and onto the main deck, looking to the south and into the face of the swirling, approaching storm. His gaze never flittered even though the *Chonjaeng Ponch'ang* was rolling back and forth considerably under the influence of the storm's waves. He went back into the bridge house.

"Put CNN on this screen and the Weather Channel on this one," he ordered Ryu, who complied immediately.

"*The storm's path has followed the projected path very closely over the last half-day or so. It looks like the predictions of hitting Washington are going to come true,*" said the voice of the Weather Channel's field reporter. On the CNN screen, an anchorwoman sat dry and warm as she reported on the storm's impending impact.

"*It's clear that Washington knows that this storm is coming but, Washington being such a busy nerve cluster, it just can't seem to shut down. Congress is still in session and the president remains in the White House. While those structures should afford plenty of protection, the bulk of Washington's residences are not fortified for such a strong storm. However, nobody seems to be leaving town and NOAA officials fear serious loss of life if people don't start evacuating,*" she said, followed by a turn to face a different camera. "*To get a feeling for what's it like out on those rough seas, our own Karl Litman is aboard the Coast Guard cutter* Yosemite. *Karl, what's it like out there?*"

"*Jan, it's getting really rough out here. I have the luxury of being able to stay inside but the brave men and women of the Yosemite get no such favors. They're out on the deck, tossing ropes over to freighter ships so they can board those ships and inspect their cargo. It's tough work and it's getting more dangerous by the minute,*" he reported.

Gwon absorbed what he could from the television reports and then studied the weather depictions on the computer displays.

"Ryu, take us forty-three miles on a heading of two-eight-eight and hold position there. When the winds hit seventy-five miles per hour we will proceed along this course," he said as he pointed to the map.

"Sir, that will take us directly into the U.S. blockade," Ryu said.

"Yes, it will."

CHAPTER 52

"Jesus, it sounds like he went through hell," Michelle said.

She and Lauren had been sitting in the coffee shop for almost an hour, hoping the rain would stop but knew that hurricane *Valerie* was making her way towards D.C.

"Yes, he did go through hell and I feel really bad for him," Lauren replied defensively. "But that doesn't mean that being with him is the right thing."

Michelle sipped her coffee. "I'm sure it would do him lots of good to have you there to support him and keep him company while he's recovering."

Lauren waved her index finger back and forth a couple of times. "I don't think so- that's just it," she said as her chest tightened, making her speech a little bit labored. "Being a martyr for somebody doesn't necessarily help them. If I stick by him just to support him and it makes me miserable, then that's not good. If I'm miserable I can't support him and he'll sense that I'm miserable and that'll make him feel bad and it'll just snowball from there and end very, very badly. I don't mean for this to sound as despicably selfish as it seems to, it's just that my relationship with Francesco was a lot like that."

"Which guy was that? Was he the guy that restored the Riva Aquaramas?" Michelle asked.

"No. That wasn't a problem. The problem with that guy, Aldo, was that not only did he not need me, I was actually getting in his way. That's another story. No, the problem with Francesco was that he didn't have a job and didn't try real hard to get or keep one. Whenever he did get one it always overwhelmed him, genuinely, and I had to help him. Not that I minded, but after a while it came to be too much, especially considering that I had a full-time job as an intelligence liaison. He had no skills to speak of and made some effort to do his job but inevitably I was the one who wound up doing the paperwork and I resented it. Even though he was really charming and did lots of things, like cooking... God, that cannoli he made was to die for... but I did stuff too, like shopping and cleaning and the tremendous amount of extra work I did for his job just filled my 'resentment sack' until that rainy afternoon when it overflowed and drowned the fledgling relationship we had."

"Huh. I hadn't thought that much about it but I can see what you mean," Barb said.

"Yeah, and that's just it with AJ. God knows, he's a much better man than Francesco will ever be, but I've got to know with AJ," she said.

"Know what?" Michelle asked.

Lauren paused and took a long sip from her coffee cup.

"I've got to know that the relationship has strong legs... I've got to know that it can go the distance," she said.

Michelle eyebrows shot up as she stared at her friend with a devilish smile and a warm feeling rushing over her.

"Lauren, are you serious?"

"Yeah, I think I am."

"Wow, I didn't think you were ready to... you know, settle; but I mean that in a good, totally hot way. So, how are you going to find out?"

"I'm not sure. As terrible as this sounds, I need for AJ to do something on his own, something significant, something that will tell me he's found that zest for life and he's willing and able to fight for it. It would only take one act, one demonstration that he's 'on the way up', so to speak, hungry for more in life- that there's a passion in there stronger than... " she paused as she visually searched the coffee shop for an analogous item, finally settling on the strengthening weather visible through the window, "— stronger than a hurricane!"

CHAPTER 53

Aboard the *Yosemite*, Captain Allison braced himself against the railings inside the bridge house.

"Cap'n, the waves are too high for boarding vessels. Dietrich just tried to toss a line over to that freighter but it snapped when she rolled away. Boarding operations are excessively dangerous in this sea state," the executive officer, Ken Dreyfuss said.

"Yeah, Ken, I think you're right. We've got to let the Operation Commander know that we can't search every vessel anymore," he said.

"I'll take care of it," Dreyfuss said. He went to the radio room and had the operator relay the situation. During the two hours that it took to get a response, the hurricane closed on their position, the winds escalated and the seas became green and tall. Dreyfuss started to make his way back up the stairs to the bridge when a large wave slammed into the *Yosemite* and caused her to heel violently to port, throwing Dreyfuss against the bulkhead. He rubbed his shoulder for a second then stuffed the report inside his jacket and grabbed both handrails for the ascent up the stairs.

On the bridge, Captain Allison had strapped himself into the 'big chair' and the rest of the bridge crew secured themselves at their stations.

"Cap'n, OpCom has ordered us to stop detaining ships. Our orders are to log the identification and class of each vessel and then order them to the nearest port where they'll be detained until such time as they can be properly searched," Dreyfuss reported.

"Makes sense to me. OK, let this freighter go. Make a log entry of its name, type, and estimated displacement," he told the Officer of the Deck.

"Aye Sir," was the brisk response.

After two hours, the *Yosemite* had logged in three vessels and a fourth was approaching. The Officer of the Deck informed Dreyfuss of the ship's approach.

"Very well," the exec replied. "Let's log it in and get this sorry bastard to safe waters."

The freighter acknowledged the radio calls from the *Yosemite* and came to a stop fifty yards away from the cutter.

* * * * *

Connelly sat on the sofa in Dixie's office and stared intensely at the television, watching the CNN report on how the U.S. naval assets were handling the ship screening as the hurricane bore down on them.

"*And now we go back to our man on the scene, Karl Litman, for a report from the Coast Guard cutter* Yosemite. *Karl, how's it going out there?*" she asked.

The screen flashed over to a dark image of a man huddled in the corner of a ship's bridge. He had braced himself against the bulkheads and managed to wrap his leg around a water pipe for support so that he could hold his microphone in one hand. Over the roar of the seventy-five mile per hour wind and the waves crashing against the ship's superstructure, he explained the situation.

"*Jan, it's gotten really, really rough out here. A couple of hours ago the Coast Guard got orders to let ships pass through without being inspected. It's too dangerous for the Coast Guard's people to jump from this ship to another one and it's too dangerous to make the freighters wait in the storm.*" he said.

"*So how are they providing security during this time of great threat from terrorists?*" she asked.

"*Jan, they've been ordered to log the name of each ship and a basic description of it and then order that ship to a designated port where it will be detained until it can be searched later.*

For example, right now we're letting a freighter pass through and the captain of the Yosemite is taking its vital information. Captain, what data are you recording for this ship?" he asked Allison.

Connelly sat forward on the edge of the sofa as he listened to the captain's response.

"This is an eighty-three foot motorized cargo vessel. We've logged that it's white with black trim on the funnels and it has a large, orange container box on its main deck," he said.

Connelly's pulse quickened when he heard that it had a container box on it. And his heart stopped when the captain finished his description.

"The ship's name is... Chonjaeng Ponch'ang. I guess it's an Asian vessel," he said.

CHAPTER 54

When Connelly got back to Station 65, he desperately tried to call Lauren. He hadn't spoken to her since he told her that he loved her and he decided that it was best to let her be alone for a while. But this was an emergency and she was in danger.

The phone lines in Washington had largely failed due to the approaching storm and cell phone service was down along much of the east coast where the storm had already battered the shore.

"Dammit!" he shouted as he tossed the receiver to the floor.

He went upstairs to his bedroom and sat on the edge of the bed with his forehead buried in his hands. In a rush, memories of Gwon's crooked, drunk smile whisked through his mind and his stomach turned with the thought. Then he thought of Lauren.

Connelly whipped open the door to his closet with his diving gear and started furiously pulling things out. Thirty minutes later, he was behind the wheel of the Range Rover racing down Highway 15 with a regulator in his mouth, the other end connected to a green dive tank filled with pure oxygen.

CHAPTER 55

The *Chonjaeng Ponch'ang* sailed slowly into Point Charles, rolling back and forth violently with the furious waves of hurricane *Valerie* battering it. The harbor was home to a dozen vessels, either prohibited from leaving or seeking refuge. The *Chonjaeng Ponch'ang* pulled into an open slip and the crew managed to drop the anchor and then eventually launch mooring lines onto the docking platform. Gwon, Ryu, and the other pirates all struggled to secure the mooring lines to the massive cleats on the deck but they eventually managed to tie the ship down enough to prevent her from smashing into the pier or running ahead and impacting the dock. They quickly secured the ship's hatches and went into the lower decks where the rolling and pitching were not quite as pronounced. At this point the seventy-five mile per hour winds of *Valerie's* outer bands were upon them and the sea churned a sickly green.

"My fellow patriots," Gwon started, "the gods of war and prosperity have paved the way for us to complete our mission. We are now within striking distance of our most hated foe and all that is left is to sever its head with our mighty sword. When the winds subside in a couple of hours we will unsheathe the mighty sword and raise it high to strike!"

His crew cheered along with him and they shouted derisive epithets towards the United States. They settled down shortly and each man found some place to wedge himself in for a while as the ship rolled about and the storm beat the deck mercilessly. The container holding the rail gun was stout and had been secured to the deck with excessive attention. Soon it would be time to fire the radioactive bomb that Ahn had spent so long constructing...

CHAPTER 56

"I have a very, very bad feeling about this," Dixie said flatly as he stared at Connelly, who was standing in front of him dressed in a full wetsuit with a regulator in his mouth.

They went from the hangar where Connelly had found Dixie back into his office. Connelly laid the oxygen cylinder next to himself on the sofa as Dixie took up a position in a folding chair facing him. There was a long, awkward silence that was broken when Connelly pulled the regulator out of his mouth to talk.

"Dixie, I've just got to do this," Connelly said.

"Do what, exactly? 'Cause from here it looks pretty dumb."

"I'm not really sure. For the longest time I tried to deny that, at some point, Gwon would reappear in my life. I felt that getting shot down in Korea was the price I had to pay to society. In every life each person has to pay a debt to society in one way or the other and I thought that was my payment had been made in full. It also seems that everyone, at some point, has to suffer some enormous hardship. I thought that spending two years as a prisoner, being beaten and starved was my hardship. Getting out of there was pure luck but I felt, having made it, that I was done with paying society. I came back to Stovall because it seemed quiet and calm and that maybe I could live out my days drinking tea, carving, and watching the sunset," he said.

"It seemed like it was working out good until Lauren showed up. How much has she got to do with it?" Dixie asked.

"Oh, Lauren's a small part and a huge part at the same time. If she hadn't knocked on my door that day somebody else would have, so I don't hold that against her. On the other hand, if she weren't in D.C. right now, honestly, I don't know if I'd be quite so motivated to act. Hell, at some point it has to be somebody else's problem, right? Do I have to solve every problem?"

"No, but you got to fix what you can. That's where I'm really wondering about this oxygen tank you've got stuck in your mouth. What the hell are you fixing to do?" Dixie asked.

Connelly took a deep breath before he began to answer. "Well, take a look at the storm track with me," he said as they moved towards the computer screen.

Ten minutes later Connelly had finished explaining his plan and Dixie slumped back in his chair.

"AJ, there's about a hundred 'if you're lucky' statements in that plan. This is suicide," Dixie said softly.

Connelly looked down at the floor for a few moments, considering Dixie's assessment of the plan. "Yeah, it has a slim chance of working. But, you know, there are a couple of things I do when I'm considering a huge decision like this. First, I compare the probability with the consequence. In this case, the probability is low but the consequence is very, very high. Given that, it's the right choice."

"And the second thing?" Dixie asked.

"I think about the two paths ahead of me. On the one hand, if I decide to try this crazy idea, I will know, one way or the other, that I did what I could to make things right. Lauren has exposed a side of me that I was ignoring or had hoped was gone. I have to give it a chance to live again. On the other hand, I could just say 'fuck it' and stay at Station 65 until the crisis is over, hoping that somebody else takes care of the problem or it fails on its own. Regardless of the outcome, I don't think I could live with myself having made that decision. Just knowing that I didn't try, even if everything turns out OK, would weigh on me forever and, frankly, my shoulders are weak and I'm tired of that kind of burden. I really don't have a choice."

"Why do I choose friends that have a conscience?" Dixie asked.

"'Because   you're really dumb," Connelly answered, smiling. "So, are you gonna help your idiotic friend kill himself or not?"

"I guess I better. This way at least I'll know you didn't kill yourself rearranging the furniture in your house," Dixie said as he got out of the chair. "I'll get the Otter started up."

CHAPTER 57

Gwon had made his way back to the chart room during the worst of the storm to check the computer data on the storm's track. He made some calculations and took his notes back into the lower hold where his crew was huddled.

"The storm is going to pass directly over us. The winds around the eyewall will be very intense but, as soon as the wall passes over us, the winds will die down to nothing. This storm's eye is very loose and not moving too fast, so we should have about one hour to deploy the gun and fire it. Be prepared! I will signal you when it is time to go on deck and prepare the weapon," Gwon said to the excited nodding of his crewmen's heads.

* * * * *

Aboard the Otter, AJ had managed to wedge himself into the copilot's seat as Dixie worked the controls. Since they were climbing above 12,500 feet they both had donned the oxygen masks provided in the cockpit of the aircraft. Dixie set his to the recommended blend of oxygen and air while Connelly set his unit to the maximum concentration of oxygen, trying to purge the nitrogen from his bloodstream so that a sudden decrease in air pressure would not result in any gas in his bloodstream to expand into a lethal embolism. The masks were equipped with voice communication capability so they could talk to each other and air traffic control but there was virtually no one manning any control towers due to the storm. Dixie made no attempt to inform the FAA of his intentions since they would not have approved it anyway.

"This Otter can just climb to a service ceiling of 26,000 feet. Fortunately, this storm's topping out at about 24,000," Dixie said through the intercom.

The storm's top was very flat, characteristic of the upper surface of a hurricane. The swirling winds still created tremendous turbulence and the Otter, even though it flew above the storm, was still being tossed violently. Connelly had managed to strap in tightly and he double-checked that his chrome-plated Colt 45 pistol was tightly locked into the holster on his right thigh. He pulled the magazine from the gun and looked at the cartridges to makes sure that he had only used the ones that he had specially prepared for this mission by painting the edges of the primer to prevent water from defusing the gunpowder in the round. He slammed the magazine back into the grip of the gun.

"How's the eye track?" Connelly asked.

Dixie took a minute to scan the display on the control panel which was jostling up and down with the rest of the airplane. "It still looks perfect. It's almost like you were meant to do this."

CHAPTER 58

"My compatriots, it is time!" Gwon shouted triumphantly. "It is time to exact revenge!"

The crew followed Gwon up the stairs through the ship which was still rolling and pitching significantly. They finally made their way to the bridge and watched as the storm's eyewall passed over their position. The one-hundred plus miles per hour wind thrashed the lines and flags on their ship and the surrounding ships. The wind howled like a pack of wolves bearing down on their very souls. The green wall of water slashed across the ship with a tremendous fury and then, in a moment's time, it became eerily quiet. The eyewall passed beyond the *Chonjaeng Ponch'ang* and they were in the still eye. The sound quieted down and the ship quickly settled to a calm rest as the water likewise came to rest.

"Now!" Gwon exhorted his crew.

Every man scrambled through the doors of the bridge and attacked their jobs with a fierce attention. Ahn and two others worked the latches on the container while Ryu and two other pirates removed the protective cover from the massive turbine generator. Within twenty minutes the container walls had been laid aside and the restraints on the gun had been removed. Ahn was already sitting at the control unit when the whine of the turbine generator signaled the impending arrival of the precious electricity needed to run the weapon. Everyone donned their ear muffs as the sound of the generator grew to a roar when it reached peak power. Ahn flipped the power switch and the control unit came to life. As he began to run the automatic systems checks, a pair of pirates retrieved the 'dirty' nuclear bomb and loaded it into the gun's breech.

High above them and fifteen miles away, Dixie and Connelly plowed through the severe turbulence over the hurricane's eyewall. Finally, with one last great heave, the Otter slipped into the calm wind in the storm's eye.

"Jesus, that was worse than when I got shot down," Connelly remarked.

"Oh, that was nothing!" Dixie replied. "I remember flying through the eye on Hugo. Man, that thing was a beast; I thought the main spars on the P-3 were gonna snap. This is nothing, you big baby."

"Yeah, well, remind me to complain to the gate agent when we arrive," Connelly joked.

CHAPTER 59

Thirty more minutes had passed and the eye of the storm was centered on the *Chonjaeng Ponch'ang*. The turbine continued to roar with a cavernous 'whoosh' of air going into the inlet, drowned out only by the staccato crackle of the exhaust. Ahn continued to monitor the controls.

"How long to fire?" Gwon yelled.

"I'm beginning to run the power-up sequence and then I have to load the targeting solution. It will take another fifteen minutes," Ahn shouted back.

Gwon grimaced as he calculated the time and the storm's track. "The other side of the eyewall will almost be here by then."

"I will work as fast as I can. However, once the weapon is powered up and the firing solution solved, the gun can still be fired in very poor weather- the delicate parts of the shot initialization will be over. The tracking servos on the barrel can compensate for even considerable pitch and roll," he assured his leader, who responded by patting him on the shoulder and then gestured for him to work as quickly as possible.

Above the storm, Connelly and Dixie soared across the eye of the storm.

"How much longer?" Connelly asked over the intercom.

"I've got to fly two orbits to find the center where the winds are zero, otherwise you'll get strangled by your own damn chute risers. I'll have you over the center of the eye ready to drop in five minutes. The storm track looks perfect- you should be over that harbor in perfect position," Dixie replied.

Dixie flew the Otter perfectly in the figure-four pattern that NOAA pilots had used for decades to find the exact center of the storm. A thin grin came across his face as he knew that he had found the calm center point of the eye. However, his face darkened when he turned to Connelly.

"AJ, are you ready for this?" Dixie asked solemnly.

"Not in the slightest," came the frank answer from Connelly.

"Well, shit, my friend. You still want to go through with this? I could have this bird turned for Bermuda in ten seconds. I understand that the weather there is perfect and the island is full of booze and women."

"It sounds great. Let's go there tomorrow- what do you say?"

"That's a deal," Dixie said.

Connelly unbuckled his harness and returned the plane's oxygen mask to its compartment as he reinserted his oxygen tank's regulator into his mouth. As he turned, Dixie grabbed his arm gently.

"Listen, AJ, I'm really looking forward to going diving with you next week. I've really enjoyed all the trips we've had together. Next week let's finish painting that railing in back; it's a lot of fun working on that heap with you," Dixie said.

Connelly looked at his feet for a second before he looked up at Dixie's face.

"Dixie, you're a real good friend. I'll see you soon. Oh, by the way, you still can't make a cup of coffee to save your life," he said with a wide grin that Dixie halfheartedly returned. Connelly slapped Dixie on the shoulder and moved towards the cockpit door. He passed through the door into the main cabin of the Otter and made his way to the jump door. He flipped the controls that allowed the air pressure inside the cabin to decrease until it matched the pressure outside, then he opened the large door on the left side of the fuselage. The wind howled and whipped around inside the cabin as Connelly held onto the door frame tightly and looked down at the colossal fury of hurricane *Valerie*. The powerful arms of the hurricane stretched for a hundred miles and the lumpy green surface betrayed the chaos inside the storm's wrath. Directly below, he could see the eye and it looked small. '*Connelly, you're a real stupid son of a bitch,*' he thought to himself. '*Well, I guess it's not such a bad way to die,*' he thought to console himself.

He hefted the oxygen tank into his left arm and clutched it very tightly. He knew that if he lost his grip on the tank it would rip the regulator out of his mouth and without the tank he'd surely drown in the water. He had tried to strap it onto his back but the parachute made that impossible and there was no way to rig up a front-side harness. He would have to hold onto it with all his might, especially when the main chute deployed and the resulting upward 'yank' would try to wrench him away from the tank. The neoprene face guard covered almost all of his exposed skin and the tips of his diving fins fluttered in the wind. He took a deep breath of oxygen and then looked up at the jump light that Dixie would flip on when the moment was right. What was seconds seemed to take hours to pass.

When the light turned bright green Connelly jumped from the plane without a moment's hesitation. The weightless sensation's comfort was overcome by the disorientation as he tumbled head-over-heels in the slipstream of the Otter. With his arms clutching the oxygen tank he was unable to stabilize himself in the conventional skydiving manner. He used his dive fins, however, to good effect and eventually stopped his tumbling and assumed a somewhat normal descent profile. Once established on the freefall he was able to slide the tank down between his legs and hold onto it with his thighs. At that point he could extend his arms and guide himself towards the dead center of the eye. He glanced at his wrist-mounted altimeter and saw that he was passing through 10,000 feet. He had decided ahead of time to pull the chute at a low altitude, six hundred feet, in order to minimize the storm's ability to carry him away from the center and into the violent wall area at the edge of the eye. His heart rate increased with each decreasing foot of altitude.

3,000 feet... 2,000 feet... 1,000 feet... *'Get ready,'* he told himself. He slid the tank back into his arms and glanced at the altimeter once more. At six feet he reached down to his left thigh and yanked the drogue chute out of a small pocket on his suit and he then immediately grasped the tank with all his strength.

The small nylon chute quickly shot above him and the cords tied to it ripped the canvas cover away from the main chute and pulled the big, beautiful nylon chute upwards. It took less than two seconds for the chute to deploy and when it did, it seized Connelly's body almost completely, arresting his motion for a split second. In that moment the inertia of the oxygen tank was too much for his grip and the tank sailed downward and ripped the regulator out of his mouth with an audible 'pop'.

'Oh fuck!' he yelled as his legs went cold with the thought of hitting the water's surface and being covered by the parachute, suffocating him only inches below the surface. The graceful canvas that was gently lowering him to Earth would soon be his coffin's lid.

'OK, this really sucks. Think fast, Connelly.'

When he got down to one-hundred feet above the surface, the winds of the storm started to carry him in a circular path. The jerks back and forth starting swinging him and his flight path looked like someone on a swing caught up in a Kansas tornado. He swung twenty feet to one side, then thirty to the other. With each oscillation he got closer to the eyewall whose impending destructive power was not lost on Connelly.

'Time to blow this pop stand!'

Recognizing that the storm wall had deadly forces in it and that landing under the canopy of the chute was equally deadly, Connelly decided to jettison the chute from fifty feet up. He seized the two buckles that secured the chute harness around him and he popped them into their unlocked positions. Immediately he sped away from the parachute and sailed forward, horizontal to the water's surface, for a good fifty feet before he impacted the surface, skipping twice like a stone on the Potomac before his body dug in and sliced under the surface.

Everything was immediately dark and the cold water bit at the exposed skin on his face. He instinctively looked down and saw the snarling faces of a dozen North Korean soldiers brandishing their bayonet-tipped rifles. His heart skipped a beat. He closed his eyes. '*AJ, it's OK. They're not real.*' He waited a moment and opened his eyes to look through the mask again and saw that the soldiers were no longer there, replaced by the slowly lightening image of turbulent sea water. The air in his lungs was becoming stale and the lack of oxygen started to burn the linings of his lungs.

The added buoyancy of the neoprene wetsuit finally pushed Connelly to the surface where he gasped for air. Bobbing up and down with each wave, he took successive breaths and finally gave his body the fresh air it had been craving. He had to watch the waves, since the buoyancy of the wetsuit would only keep his head above water *on average*. When a wave crest came by it passed over his head and he had to time his breathing just right.

After a minute of breathing, he surveyed his surroundings and saw that he was about fifty yards from the nearest pier and he began paddling that way in the roiling sea. As he got closer, he began to synchronize his movements to the wave's rise and fall. He had to be careful to not be slammed against the wooden piling too hard and lose consciousness. Up and down... wait... up and down... wait...

When the moment was right, he surged forward just as the crest of the wave he was on drove forward onto a piling. The wave thrust him onto the wooden pole and he clung to it like a gecko as the water fell away beneath him. He managed to get his finned feet wrapped around the pole and inched his way up as each successive wave had less and less influence on his stability. When he reached the top he managed to swing his torso up onto the concrete slab and he rolled onto his back for a moment's rest.

After thirty seconds he sat up, took off the fins, and got to his feet. The winds were starting to pick back up considerably, already at twenty-five miles per hour. He ran down the walkway to the main part of the pier, already surveying the ships that were in the Point Charles Harbor. There were about two dozens ships, mostly cargo ships of moderate size. He was presently near one end of the harbor so he ran quickly down to the end, trying to stay hidden by the various structures as much as possible. The ship on the very end had *Ocean Hauler* painted on its bow and its deck was barren, so he moved to the next ship.

"The wind is picking up, Ahn. How much longer?" Gwon asked impatiently.

"The start sequence is completed and I am entering the data for the firing solution now. The computer is calculating the azimuth, elevation, and rail speeds for the shot. It will be ready momentarily," he answered.

The ship had begun to roll vigorously as the center of the eye moved off their position. Gwon looked at the wall of the eye and could see failure in its roiling green morass. He found his fingers scratching the wooden railing he was clutching, knowing that this was his only chance; as soon as the storm passed the Coast Guard and, undoubtedly, other agencies would be on top of them.

The *Montgomery Johnson* was a small petrol carrier with tank hatches being the only thing across her deck. The rain had gotten heavier and Connelly was having a hard time seeing details on the ships clearly. The wind continued to ramp up and debris from the shore sailed about. A few palm fronds and a flock of paper rubbish swirled around the harbor. He ran to the next ship, ducking his head and using his hands as an awning to keep some of the rain out of his eyes. He had examined nineteen of the twenty-four ships when his eyes caught sight of the black lettering brazenly painted on the port bow of the twentieth ship. The letters were Korean, but they were two of the dozen or so words he could read in Korean and they spelled out *Chonjaeng Ponch'ang*. He immediately ducked behind a storage shed that hadn't been blown down yet and pulled the Colt 45 from its holster. He looked straight down, trying to breathe normally and slow his heart rate. Gwon was aboard that ship, murder in his heart, and Connelly was going to have to stop him. He slowly looked back up at the cargo ship and he could see one sentry on the main deck of the ship making a lackluster circuit around the bow, no doubt wishing to be inside as the rain began to pour and the winds howl. The ship was rocking back and forth and with each sideways surge the massive mooring lines strained at their cleats. It would be a rough ride, but Connelly could think of no other way to board the vessel. He cycled the slide on the Colt to chamber a round and then he timed his dash down the pier to minimize the sentry's chance of detecting him.

'Slap! Slap! Slap!' his feet sounded as he sprinted down the concrete jetty, then ducking behind the steel cleat. He scanned the weather deck of the ship. He looked for the sentry on the bow but didn't see him. '*Must be on the starboard side. Probably staying dry,*' he thought to himself. He tracked his gaze aft and saw a second sentry looking over the transom on the stern of the ship. He didn't seem to be moving much, mostly watching for someone approaching by sea. '*Hah! He doesn't think anybody would be stupid enough to parachute in and siege the ship on foot!*' Connelly thought sarcastically to himself. As he did, he noticed that the sound of the wind had dramatically increased. But then he thought that it wasn't just the wind, it was something else... some high pitched sound was now mixing with the turbulent howl of the hurricane's quickly-approaching eyewall. He holstered his handgun and slipped around the cleat to grab the massive mooring line. Hand-over-hand, he made his way from the jetty towards the ship. With each roll, the line tightened and then relaxed. He had to hang on tightly when the rope went from slack to taught since it propelled him upwards quickly enough to throw him if he wasn't careful. He kept his eyes on the gunwales of the ship as he approached but he didn't see either of the sentries. He reached one arm towards the hull of the *Chonjaeng Ponch'ang* and grabbed the lip of the scupper plate hole. When he had a firm grip, he let go of the rope altogether and hung on the lip of the scupper hole. On a ship the size of the *Chonjaeng Ponch'ang* he could fit through the hole and managed to do so, slipping onto the main deck. He quickly scooted aboard and hid himself between a davit motor housing and a fire extinguisher storage bin so that he could redraw his weapon and take stock of the sentries' positions. Not seeing either, he made his way aft and noticed the additional sound was loud and high, like a jet engine. This was definitely the right place and Gwon was getting close to doing whatever it was he was planning. Connelly had to move quickly. He spotted the sentry looking the other way and took the opportunity to sprint towards the man, closing the distance between them in only a second. When he was only ten feet away he trained the Colt on the man's chest and ripped off two shots. The first caught him in the chest and the second in his shoulder, the man collapsing to the deck. Connelly quickly ducked out of sight and looked around to see if the shot had attracted any attention. He didn't see anyone so he made his way to the fallen man, grabbed his ankles, and struggled to drag him out of sight across the rolling deck.

Just as he had the man almost concealed behind a hatchway, a thudding sound, immediately followed by a metallic rattling slapped him. The first sentry's machine gun had thrown a dozen rounds at Connelly but none made their mark as the man was still some distance away and firing from his hip. Connelly slipped through the hatchway and immediately ducked behind the steel door. He peered out through the crack between the hatch and the bulkhead, waiting for the pursuer to follow him.

The room erupted with the sound of bullets striking steel hull plating as the sentry hosed down the hatchway with 7.62mm hollow point rounds blazing from his AK-47. When his magazine was empty, the man stepped to the threshold of the hatch to peer in. The only thing he saw was the single muzzle flash from the Colt 45 as a round jumped from the gun, passed through the crack between the hatch and the bulkhead, and blew a hole in the man's head. The melange of liquid and solid detritus on the deck made Connelly's stomach turn and he had to look away. Fortunately, the rain and wind cleared the mess fairly quickly or at least spread it into a less-recognizable discoloration of the deckplating.

Connelly ejected the magazine from the Colt to count the rounds. 'Four in the mag and one in the chamber. Five shots left,' Connelly noted. As he turned to leave the compartment he saw that the sentry's rifle had fallen to the deck but it looked undamaged. He picked up the weapon and grabbed a second magazine from the corpse's bandolier and exchanged it for the emptied one in the gun. He cycled the slide on the AK.

"What the hell was that?" Gwon shouted at the three other pirates.

They immediately drew their weapons and moved towards the aft part of the ship. Two of the men took a narrow passageway leading from the starboard side of the ship to the port side and turned aft when they were on the other side of the ship. They took two steps forward and then caught sight of one of their compatriots lying on the deck, mangled and bloody. For a moment they hesitated in shock and that's when

Connelly opened fire with the machine gun, managing to get six of the twenty rounds he fired onto the target. The two pirates twisted and flailed in their last moments and managed to fire off a couple of unaimed rounds harmlessly into the rainy sky.

Connelly heard a sound through the cacophony that sent a chill down his spine. It was the unmistakable nasal-centric sound of the man that had tortured him for almost two years. He turned towards Gwon's voice and struggled to move each leg forward, as though the sound of Gwon's voice was turning his legs into concrete. Nevertheless, Connelly managed to cross over to the starboard side of the ship, one deck higher on the superstructure than Gwon and Ahn. He was close enough to hear Gwon's voice.

"Ahn, we must fire now!" he shouted.

"Yes Sir, the solution is solved and I just activated the firing sequence," Ahn excitedly replied.

Connelly wasn't sure what Gwon had said but Connelly deduced that the massive machine next to him was a weapon of tremendous destructive power and Gwon had just told him to fire it. It was 'now or never' time.

He leapt over the rail and slammed onto the deck only ten feet away from the control console. Ahn, startled, sprung to his feet and charged at Connelly. Instinctively, Connelly yanked the Colt and blasted two rounds into the technician's chest. His forward progress halted and the man meekly crumpled to the deck.

"Mister Johnson!" Gwon shouted with a mixture of surprise and delight that sickened Connelly. "So nice of you to join me in my moment of triumph! I didn't know you were still alive but I am so pleased that you are. Awful weather we're having, isn't it?" he sardonically asked.

Connelly didn't reply but raised his pistol to aim at Gwon's head. 'Three rounds left,' he reminded himself. He swallowed hard and then his shoulder started to burn with pain. It seemed backwards that the sound of the AK-47 from the last pirate's rifle reached him seconds after the lead slug ripped through his shoulder and ribcage. With unadulterated speed and conviction, Connelly whirled around and saw the black-clad pirate running towards him, the flashes from his rifle lighting his face like a strobe. Connelly trained the Colt on his chest and broke off three quick rounds that all struck him in the chest. The pirate collapsed in an uncoordinated flop and his body rolled off the deck as the ship heaved to starboard.

A guffaw pierced the roar and whine of the storm and the turbine generator, wrangling Connelly's attention. He turned to face Gwon and realized that he had expended the rounds in the gun.

"It's too bad that you failed, Mister Johnson," Gwon said.

Connelly looked at Ahn, the dead operator. "Did I?" he asked.

Gwon saw that he was looking at the dead man, thinking that his absence would prevent the shot from being made. "Unfortunately, for you, he already started the firing sequence. It can't be stopped now. You could even kill me but everyone in Washington would still die from radiation poisoning all because you were too late and too weak to stop me. You are really pathetic, Mister Johnson. Look at you- bleeding from head to toe now, just as you did each day in my camp. You may have gotten away once but you had to know that you could never beat me, not in the end. Now you are bleeding and dying and I am going to throw you into the ocean just like the sewage we pump from the bilge. You can't stop me."

Gwon began striding confidently towards Connelly who was now down on one knee, the pain of the bullet wounds drawing down his strength as the inevitable destruction of Washington D.C. and his own demise weighed him down. The eyewall closed on him, a terrifying backdrop to the madman Gwon who strode closer and closer.

"You see, Mister Johnson, I have it all figured out and I haven't forgotten anything." He glanced at the display on the rail gun's control unit. "The gun will fire in fifteen seconds and there's no way to stop it. The plan is complete and I won. I won!" he shouted as he stood over Connelly.

Then Connelly thought of Lauren. Her gorgeous black hair gently blowing in the wind of a thousand fantasies, her satin skin under his fingertips, her soft lips, and the surge from his heart that suddenly powered his legs and cleared his mind.

He looked up at Gwon. "Yes, you are very clever," he said as Gwon's smile ripped from ear to ear. "But there are two things you don't get."

"And what are those?" Gwon asked as though speaking to a child.

"One, all the torture I endured at your hands taught me how to absorb endless pain and keep functioning," he said, followed by a lightning-quick motion in which he drove his right hand into Gwon's crotch, crushing his testicles in his grip. With his left hand he strangled Gwon's throat. As his face contorted in pain, Gwon moved one hand to try to release the grip on his crotch and the other to defend against the suffocating grip with little effect in either case.

"And the second thing," Connelly said as he pulled Gwon's throat down towards him and then lifting the man high above his head like a weight lifter performing a standing press with a barbell. Connelly looked up into the terrified eyes of his once-captor. "My name is Connelly!"

With that declaration made, Connelly began to run down the deck with Gwon still lofted over his head, desperately trying to detach himself from Connelly's lethal grip. He saw the rail gun's coils glow with power as the launch was on the brink of its ultimate phase. Gwon knew that he might die in a moment but at least the launch will be successful and he will have triumphed in the eyes of General Seong, North Korea, and himself. '*I will be a martyr- school children will sing songs of my bravery. Nothing can stop my legacy now!*' *The only thing that could stop the gun now would be a total loss of power and there's no way he could stop the generator now...*' Gwon thought as his eyes rolled to the generator, which was fast approaching. His heart filled with dread. '*He couldn't...*' was the last thought Gwon had before Connelly hurled the man's body like a javelin into the inlet of the massive engine with its razor-sharp compressor blades spinning at 15,000 rpm.

There was a crunching sound at first, followed a puff of black smoke, and then an enormous, putrid cloud of black smoke as the rapid slowing of the compressor marked its imminent shutdown. The control panel's warning lights lit up and the gun's accelerator coils went cold. The control panel only had enough electricity left to indicate that the shot had failed and then the unit itself shutdown, its displays darkened. Connelly fell to his knees and clutched his head in his hands as the rain from the hurricane came down in droves.

EPILOGUE

Connelly could sense that he was lying down and that someone was in the room. His head hurt tremendously, as though a vice were securely clamped across his temples. However, he was dry and the light covers over him kept him comfortable.

"Yeah, right there, keeled right over. I threw an old cardboard box over him and went to bed."

Connelly heard the voice but couldn't immediately place it.

"That's really funny. I'd love to see him that soused."

That voice Connelly recognized. It was Lauren's.

I had to brew a 93-octane pot of coffee the next morning."

And that was Dixie Walker's voice.

"And it was terrible. You can fly the hell out of an airplane but you can't make coffee worth a damn," Connelly said with a somewhat labored voice. He was immediately rewarded with a warm squeeze of his hand by the unmistakably comforting grip of Lauren's soft skin.

"AJ, sweetheart, are you there?" she asked softly.

It took a few seconds for Connelly to crack his eyelids open and a few more seconds for his eyes to focus on the interior of the hospital room. He quickly tracked his sight over to the beautiful vision of Lauren's face.

"Yeah, I'm here... wherever 'here' is. What the crap happened? Where am I?"

"You, my insane friend, are at GW University Hospital," Dixie said as he rose and came to the side of the bed. "You really need to learn to wear a seatbelt. You fell out of my airplane right into the ocean. Then the ship... and the Bradley. Geez, it's a miracle you're alive," he said with a broad grin.

"Ship? Bradley? What are you talking about, you crazy old bastard?" he groggily asked.

Dixie recognized that Connelly's playful condescension was a good sign and took the opportunity give him and Lauren some time together. He gave Connelly a careful pat on the shoulder. "You recover, my friend. I'll see you back at Station 65," he said as he waved to Lauren and strolled out of the room.

Lauren carefully sat on the edge of the hospital bed and looked at Connelly intently but with a big smile.

"What was he talking about?" Connelly asked.

"Well, I got word through an FAA controller that some *idiot* had parachuted into Port Charles in the middle of the hurricane. Knowing that Dixie was an ex-NOAA hurricane hunter pilot and that you're, well, an incredible man, I figured it had to be you."

"So how did I get here?" Connelly asked.

"Well, I immediately tried to get to Point Charles but it took a few hours and I had to tear into a few people to get transportation down there. It's tough, you know, as a hurricane's passing through, to hail a cab. I finally got a colonel in the National Guard to have a Bradley pick me up and drive me down there. Point Charles was completely destroyed- a good thing we were in a 'fighting vehicle'. It took a long time but we found the *Chonjaeng Ponch'ang* and the soldier from the Bradley and I climbed into the ship and eventually found you."

"Climbed into it? How did you do that?" AJ asked.

"Well, it had been thrown onto the dock by the storm so it really was more like climbing a jungle gym than boarding a ship. We found you crumpled up next to a diesel engine down about three decks. We managed to get you back to the Bradley and to the hospital."

"Wow. I don't remember any of that," AJ said as he closed his eyes with mournful fatigue.

"We found a bunch of dead Koreans onboard but nobody has been able to identify Gwon's body. Did he get away?"

"No, he didn't," Connelly said as he slipped his arm onto Lauren's thigh.

"Careful, Mister! You've got about six-hundred stitches in you and enough plaster on you to make a life-size copy of the Parthenon," she said playfully.

A rap on the door interrupted them as a nurse walked into the room with a tray. Connelly slid his hand off of Lauren's leg, anticipating her getting up which, surprisingly, she did not.

"Um, are you going... back to D.C. or somewhere?" Connelly asked softly with a wrinkled brow.

"Nope."

"You're staying?" he asked.

"Yes, I'm staying. I'm staying for good," she answered.

Printed in the United States
68467LVS00001B/10